COLLECTED WORKS OF
MARY ELEANOR WILKINS FREEMAN

COLLECTED WORKS OF
MARY ELEANOR WILKINS FREEMAN

THE WIND IN THE ROSE-BUSH AND OTHER STORIES OF THE SUPERNATURAL,
AND
THE YATES PRIDE

BIBLIOBAZAAR

COLLECTED WORKS OF
MARY ELEANOR WILKINS FREEMAN

CONTENTS

THE WIND IN THE ROSE-BUSH

THE YATES PRIDE

THE WIND IN THE ROSE-BUSH

And Other Stories Of The Supernatural

THE WIND IN THE ROSE-BUSH

Ford Village has no railroad station, being on the other side of the river from Porter's Falls, and accessible only by the ford which gives it its name, and a ferry line.

The ferry-boat was waiting when Rebecca Flint got off the train with her bag and lunch basket. When she and her small trunk were safely embarked she sat stiff and straight and calm in the ferry-boat as it shot swiftly and smoothly across stream. There was a horse attached to a light country wagon on board, and he pawed the deck uneasily. His owner stood near, with a wary eye upon him, although he was chewing, with as dully reflective an expression as a cow. Beside Rebecca sat a woman of about her own age, who kept looking at her with furtive curiosity; her husband, short and stout and saturnine, stood near her. Rebecca paid no attention to either of them. She was tall and spare and pale, the type of a spinster, yet with rudimentary lines and expressions of matronhood. She all unconsciously held her shawl, rolled up in a canvas bag, on her left hip, as if it had been a child. She wore a settled frown of dissent at life, but it was the frown of a mother who regarded life as a froward child, rather than as an overwhelming fate.

The other woman continued staring at her; she was mildly stupid, except for an over-developed curiosity which made her at times sharp beyond belief. Her eyes glittered, red spots came on her flaccid cheeks; she kept opening her mouth to speak, making little abortive motions. Finally she could endure it no longer; she nudged Rebecca boldly.

"A pleasant day," said she.

Rebecca looked at her and nodded coldly.

"Yes, very," she assented.

"Have you come far?"

"I have come from Michigan."

"Oh!" said the woman, with awe. "It's a long way," she remarked presently.

"Yes, it is," replied Rebecca, conclusively.

Still the other woman was not daunted; there was something which she determined to know, possibly roused thereto by a vague sense of incongruity in the other's appearance. "It's a long ways to come and leave a family," she remarked with painful slyness.

"I ain't got any family to leave," returned Rebecca shortly.

"Then you ain't—"

"No, I ain't."

"Oh!" said the woman.

Rebecca looked straight ahead at the race of the river.

It was a long ferry. Finally Rebecca herself waxed unexpectedly loquacious. She turned to the other woman and inquired if she knew John Dent's widow who lived in Ford Village. "Her husband died about three years ago," said she, by way of detail.

The woman started violently. She turned pale, then she flushed; she cast a strange glance at her husband, who was regarding both women with a sort of stolid keenness.

"Yes, I guess I do," faltered the woman finally.

"Well, his first wife was my sister," said Rebecca with the air of one imparting important intelligence.

"Was she?" responded the other woman feebly. She glanced at her husband with an expression of doubt and terror, and he shook his head forbiddingly.

"I'm going to see her, and take my niece Agnes home with me," said Rebecca.

Then the woman gave such a violent start that she noticed it.

"What is the matter?" she asked.

"Nothin', I guess," replied the woman, with eyes on her husband, who was slowly shaking his head, like a Chinese toy.

"Is my niece sick?" asked Rebecca with quick suspicion.

"No, she ain't sick," replied the woman with alacrity, then she caught her breath with a gasp.

"When did you see her?"

"Let me see; I ain't seen her for some little time," replied the woman. Then she caught her breath again.

"She ought to have grown up real pretty, if she takes after my sister. She was a real pretty woman," Rebecca said wistfully.

"Yes, I guess she did grow up pretty," replied the woman in a trembling voice.

"What kind of a woman is the second wife?"

The woman glanced at her husband's warning face. She continued to gaze at him while she replied in a choking voice to Rebecca:

"I—guess she's a nice woman," she replied. "I—don't know, I—guess so. I—don't see much of her."

"I felt kind of hurt that John married again so quick," said Rebecca; "but I suppose he wanted his house kept, and Agnes wanted care. I wasn't so situated that I could take her when her mother died. I had my own mother to care for, and I was school-teaching. Now mother has gone, and my uncle died six months ago and left me quite a little property, and I've given up my school, and I've come for Agnes. I guess she'll be glad to go with me, though I suppose her stepmother is a good woman, and has always done for her."

The man's warning shake at his wife was fairly portentous.

"I guess so," said she.

"John always wrote that she was a beautiful woman," said Rebecca.

Then the ferry-boat grated on the shore.

John Dent's widow had sent a horse and wagon to meet her sister-in-law. When the woman and her husband went down the road, on which Rebecca in the wagon with her trunk soon passed them, she said reproachfully:

"Seems as if I'd ought to have told her, Thomas."

"Let her find it out herself," replied the man. "Don't you go to burnin' your fingers in other folks' puddin', Maria."

"Do you s'pose she'll see anything?" asked the woman with a spasmodic shudder and a terrified roll of her eyes.

"See!" returned her husband with stolid scorn. "Better be sure there's anything to see."

"Oh, Thomas, they say—"

"Lord, ain't you found out that what they say is mostly lies?"

"But if it should be true, and she's a nervous woman, she might be scared enough to lose her wits," said his wife, staring uneasily after Rebecca's erect figure in the wagon disappearing over the crest of the hilly road.

"Wits that so easy upset ain't worth much," declared the man. "You keep out of it, Maria."

Rebecca in the meantime rode on in the wagon, beside a flaxen-headed boy, who looked, to her understanding, not very bright. She asked him a question, and he paid no attention. She repeated it, and he responded with a bewildered and incoherent grunt. Then she let him alone, after making sure that he knew how to drive straight.

They had traveled about half a mile, passed the village square, and gone a short distance beyond, when the boy drew up with a sudden Whoa! before a very prosperous-looking house. It had been one of the aboriginal cottages of the vicinity, small and white, with a roof extending on one side over a piazza, and a tiny "L" jutting out in the rear, on the right hand. Now the cottage was transformed by dormer windows, a bay window on the piazzaless side, a carved railing down the front steps, and a modern hard-wood door.

"Is this John Dent's house?" asked Rebecca.

The boy was as sparing of speech as a philosopher. His only response was in flinging the reins over the horse's back, stretching out one foot to the shaft, and leaping out of the wagon, then going around to the rear for the trunk. Rebecca got out and went toward the house. Its white paint had a new gloss; its blinds were an immaculate apple green; the lawn was trimmed as smooth as velvet, and it was dotted with scrupulous groups of hydrangeas and cannas.

"I always understood that John Dent was well-to-do," Rebecca reflected comfortably. "I guess Agnes will have considerable. I've got enough, but it will come in handy for her schooling. She can have advantages."

The boy dragged the trunk up the fine gravel-walk, but before he reached the steps leading up to the piazza, for the house stood on a terrace, the front door opened and a fair, frizzled head of a very large and handsome woman appeared. She held up her black silk skirt, disclosing voluminous ruffles of starched embroidery, and waited for Rebecca. She smiled placidly, her pink, double-chinned face widened and dimpled, but her blue eyes were wary and calculating. She extended her hand as Rebecca climbed the steps.

"This is Miss Flint, I suppose," said she.

"Yes, ma'am," replied Rebecca, noticing with bewilderment a curious expression compounded of fear and defiance on the other's face.

"Your letter only arrived this morning," said Mrs. Dent, in a steady voice. Her great face was a uniform pink, and her china-blue eyes were at once aggressive and veiled with secrecy.

"Yes, I hardly thought you'd get my letter," replied Rebecca. "I felt as if I could not wait to hear from you before I came. I supposed you would be so situated that you could have me a little while without putting you out too much, from what John used to write me about his circumstances, and when I had that money so unexpected I felt as if I must come for Agnes. I suppose you will be willing to give her up. You know she's my own blood, and of course she's no relation to you, though you must have got attached to her. I know from her picture what a sweet girl she must be, and John always said she looked like her own mother, and Grace was a beautiful woman, if she was my sister."

Rebecca stopped and stared at the other woman in amazement and alarm. The great handsome blonde creature stood speechless, livid, gasping, with her hand to her heart, her lips parted in a horrible caricature of a smile.

"Are you sick!" cried Rebecca, drawing near. "Don't you want me to get you some water!"

Then Mrs. Dent recovered herself with a great effort. "It is nothing," she said. "I am subject to—spells. I am over it now. Won't you come in, Miss Flint?"

As she spoke, the beautiful deep-rose colour suffused her face, her blue eyes met her visitor's with the opaqueness of turquoise—with a revelation of blue, but a concealment of all behind.

Rebecca followed her hostess in, and the boy, who had waited quiescently, climbed the steps with the trunk. But before they entered the door a strange thing happened. On the upper terrace close to the piazza-post, grew a great rose-bush, and on it, late in the season though it was, one small red, perfect rose.

Rebecca looked at it, and the other woman extended her hand with a quick gesture. "Don't you pick that rose!" she brusquely cried.

Rebecca drew herself up with stiff dignity.

"I ain't in the habit of picking other folks' roses without leave," said she.

As Rebecca spoke she started violently, and lost sight of her resentment, for something singular happened. Suddenly the rose-bush was agitated violently as if by a gust of wind, yet it was a remarkably still day. Not a leaf of the hydrangea standing on the terrace close to the rose trembled.

"What on earth—" began Rebecca, then she stopped with a gasp at the sight of the other woman's face. Although a face, it gave somehow the impression of a desperately clutched hand of secrecy.

"Come in!" said she in a harsh voice, which seemed to come forth from her chest with no intervention of the organs of speech. "Come into the house. I'm getting cold out here."

"What makes that rose-bush blow so when their isn't any wind?" asked Rebecca, trembling with vague horror, yet resolute.

"I don't see as it is blowing," returned the woman calmly. And as she spoke, indeed, the bush was quiet.

"It was blowing," declared Rebecca.

"It isn't now," said Mrs. Dent. "I can't try to account for everything that blows out-of-doors. I have too much to do."

She spoke scornfully and confidently, with defiant, unflinching eyes, first on the bush, then on Rebecca, and led the way into the house.

"It looked queer," persisted Rebecca, but she followed, and also the boy with the trunk.

Rebecca entered an interior, prosperous, even elegant, according to her simple ideas. There were Brussels carpets, lace curtains, and plenty of brilliant upholstery and polished wood.

"You're real nicely situated," remarked Rebecca, after she had become a little accustomed to her new surroundings and the two women were seated at the tea-table.

Mrs. Dent stared with a hard complacency from behind her silver-plated service. "Yes, I be," said she.

"You got all the things new?" said Rebecca hesitatingly, with a jealous memory of her dead sister's bridal furnishings.

"Yes," said Mrs. Dent; "I was never one to want dead folks' things, and I had money enough of my own, so I wasn't beholden to John. I had the old duds put up at auction. They didn't bring much."

"I suppose you saved some for Agnes. She'll want some of her poor mother's things when she is grown up," said Rebecca with some indignation.

The defiant stare of Mrs. Dent's blue eyes waxed more intense. "There's a few things up garret," said she.

"She'll be likely to value them," remarked Rebecca. As she spoke she glanced at the window. "Isn't it most time for her to be coming home?" she asked.

"Most time," answered Mrs. Dent carelessly; "but when she gets over to Addie Slocum's she never knows when to come home."

"Is Addie Slocum her intimate friend?"

"Intimate as any."

"Maybe we can have her come out to see Agnes when she's living with me," said Rebecca wistfully. "I suppose she'll be likely to be homesick at first."

"Most likely," answered Mrs. Dent.

"Does she call you mother?" Rebecca asked.

"No, she calls me Aunt Emeline," replied the other woman shortly. "When did you say you were going home?"

"In about a week, I thought, if she can be ready to go so soon," answered Rebecca with a surprised look.

She reflected that she would not remain a day longer than she could help after such an inhospitable look and question.

"Oh, as far as that goes," said Mrs. Dent, "it wouldn't make any difference about her being ready. You could go home whenever you felt that you must, and she could come afterward."

"Alone?"

"Why not? She's a big girl now, and you don't have to change cars."

"My niece will go home when I do, and not travel alone; and if I can't wait here for her, in the house that used to be her mother's and my sister's home, I'll go and board somewhere," returned Rebecca with warmth.

"Oh, you can stay here as long as you want to. You're welcome," said Mrs. Dent.

Then Rebecca started. "There she is!" she declared in a trembling, exultant voice. Nobody knew how she longed to see the girl.

"She isn't as late as I thought she'd be," said Mrs. Dent, and again that curious, subtle change passed over her face, and again it settled into that stony impassiveness.

Rebecca stared at the door, waiting for it to open. "Where is she?" she asked presently.

"I guess she's stopped to take off her hat in the entry," suggested Mrs. Dent.

Rebecca waited. "Why don't she come? It can't take her all this time to take off her hat."

For answer Mrs. Dent rose with a stiff jerk and threw open the door.

"Agnes!" she called. "Agnes!" Then she turned and eyed Rebecca. "She ain't there."

"I saw her pass the window," said Rebecca in bewilderment.

"You must have been mistaken."

"I know I did," persisted Rebecca.

"You couldn't have."

"I did. I saw first a shadow go over the ceiling, then I saw her in the glass there"—she pointed to a mirror over the sideboard opposite—"and then the shadow passed the window."

"How did she look in the glass?"

"Little and light-haired, with the light hair kind of tossing over her forehead."

"You couldn't have seen her."

"Was that like Agnes?"

"Like enough; but of course you didn't see her. You've been thinking so much about her that you thought you did."

"You thought YOU did."

"I thought I saw a shadow pass the window, but I must have been mistaken. She didn't come in, or we would have seen her before now. I knew it was too early for her to get home from Addie Slocum's, anyhow."

When Rebecca went to bed Agnes had not returned. Rebecca had resolved that she would not retire until the girl came, but she was very tired, and she reasoned with herself that she was foolish. Besides, Mrs. Dent suggested that Agnes might go to the church social with Addie Slocum. When Rebecca suggested that she be sent for and told that her aunt had come, Mrs. Dent laughed meaningly.

"I guess you'll find out that a young girl ain't so ready to leave a sociable, where there's boys, to see her aunt," said she.

"She's too young," said Rebecca incredulously and indignantly.

"She's sixteen," replied Mrs. Dent; "and she's always been great for the boys."

"She's going to school four years after I get her before she thinks of boys," declared Rebecca.

"We'll see," laughed the other woman.

After Rebecca went to bed, she lay awake a long time listening for the sound of girlish laughter and a boy's voice under her window; then she fell asleep.

The next morning she was down early. Mrs. Dent, who kept no servants, was busily preparing breakfast.

"Don't Agnes help you about breakfast?" asked Rebecca.

"No, I let her lay," replied Mrs. Dent shortly.

"What time did she get home last night?"

"She didn't get home."

"What?"

"She didn't get home. She stayed with Addie. She often does."

"Without sending you word?"

"Oh, she knew I wouldn't worry."

"When will she be home?"

"Oh, I guess she'll be along pretty soon."

Rebecca was uneasy, but she tried to conceal it, for she knew of no good reason for uneasiness. What was there to occasion alarm in the fact of one young girl staying overnight with another? She could not eat much breakfast. Afterward she went out on the little piazza, although her hostess strove furtively to stop her.

"Why don't you go out back of the house? It's real pretty—a view over the river," she said.

"I guess I'll go out here," replied Rebecca. She had a purpose: to watch for the absent girl.

Presently Rebecca came hustling into the house through the sitting-room, into the kitchen where Mrs. Dent was cooking.

"That rose-bush!" she gasped.

Mrs. Dent turned and faced her.

"What of it?"

"It's a-blowing."

"What of it?"

"There isn't a mite of wind this morning."

Mrs. Dent turned with an inimitable toss of her fair head. "If you think I can spend my time puzzling over such nonsense as—" she began, but Rebecca interrupted her with a cry and a rush to the door.

"There she is now!" she cried. She flung the door wide open, and curiously enough a breeze came in and her own gray hair tossed, and a paper blew off the table to the floor with a loud rustle, but there was nobody in sight.

"There's nobody here," Rebecca said.

She looked blankly at the other woman, who brought her rolling-pin down on a slab of pie-crust with a thud.

"I didn't hear anybody," she said calmly.

"I SAW SOMEBODY PASS THAT WINDOW!"

"You were mistaken again."

"I KNOW I saw somebody."

"You couldn't have. Please shut that door."

Rebecca shut the door. She sat down beside the window and looked out on the autumnal yard, with its little curve of footpath to the kitchen door.

"What smells so strong of roses in this room?" she said presently. She sniffed hard.

"I don't smell anything but these nutmegs."

"It is not nutmeg."

"I don't smell anything else."

"Where do you suppose Agnes is?"

"Oh, perhaps she has gone over the ferry to Porter's Falls with Addie. She often does. Addie's got an aunt over there, and Addie's got a cousin, a real pretty boy."

"You suppose she's gone over there?"

"Mebbe. I shouldn't wonder."

"When should she be home?"

"Oh, not before afternoon."

Rebecca waited with all the patience she could muster. She kept reassuring herself, telling herself that it was all natural, that the other woman could not help it, but she made up her mind that if Agnes did not return that afternoon she should be sent for.

When it was four o'clock she started up with resolution. She had been furtively watching the onyx clock on the sitting-room mantel; she had timed herself. She had said that if Agnes was not home by that time she should demand that she be sent for. She rose and stood before Mrs. Dent, who looked up coolly from her embroidery.

"I've waited just as long as I'm going to," she said. "I've come 'way from Michigan to see my own sister's daughter and take her home with me. I've been here ever since yesterday—twenty-four hours—and I haven't seen her. Now I'm going to. I want her sent for."

Mrs. Dent folded her embroidery and rose.

"Well, I don't blame you," she said. "It is high time she came home. I'll go right over and get her myself."

Rebecca heaved a sigh of relief. She hardly knew what she had suspected or feared, but she knew that her position had been one of antagonism if not accusation, and she was sensible of relief.

"I wish you would," she said gratefully, and went back to her chair, while Mrs. Dent got her shawl and her little white head-tie. "I wouldn't trouble you, but I do feel as if I couldn't wait any longer to see her," she remarked apologetically.

"Oh, it ain't any trouble at all," said Mrs. Dent as she went out. "I don't blame you; you have waited long enough."

Rebecca sat at the window watching breathlessly until Mrs. Dent came stepping through the yard alone. She ran to the door and saw, hardly noticing it this time, that the rose-bush was again violently agitated, yet with no wind evident elsewhere.

"Where is she?" she cried.

Mrs. Dent laughed with stiff lips as she came up the steps over the terrace. "Girls will be girls," said she. "She's gone with Addie to Lincoln. Addie's got an uncle who's conductor on the train, and lives there, and he got 'em passes, and they're goin' to stay to Addie's Aunt Margaret's a few days. Mrs. Slocum said Agnes didn't have time to come over and ask me before the train went, but she took it on herself to say it would be all right, and—"

"Why hadn't she been over to tell you?" Rebecca was angry, though not suspicious. She even saw no reason for her anger.

"Oh, she was putting up grapes. She was coming over just as soon as she got the black off her hands. She heard I had company, and her hands were a sight. She was holding them over sulphur matches."

"You say she's going to stay a few days?" repeated Rebecca dazedly.

"Yes; till Thursday, Mrs. Slocum said."

"How far is Lincoln from here?"

"About fifty miles. It'll be a real treat to her. Mrs. Slocum's sister is a real nice woman."

"It is goin' to make it pretty late about my goin' home."

"If you don't feel as if you could wait, I'll get her ready and send her on just as soon as I can," Mrs. Dent said sweetly.

"I'm going to wait," said Rebecca grimly.

The two women sat down again, and Mrs. Dent took up her embroidery.

"Is there any sewing I can do for her?" Rebecca asked finally in a desperate way. "If I can get her sewing along some—"

Mrs. Dent arose with alacrity and fetched a mass of white from the closet. "Here," she said, "if you want to sew the lace on this nightgown. I was going to put her to it, but she'll be glad enough to get rid of it. She ought to have this and one more before she goes. I don't like to send her away without some good underclothing."

Rebecca snatched at the little white garment and sewed feverishly.

That night she wakened from a deep sleep a little after midnight and lay a minute trying to collect her faculties and explain to herself what she was listening to. At last she discovered that it was the then popular strains of "The Maiden's Prayer" floating up through the floor from the piano in the sitting-room below. She jumped up, threw a shawl over her nightgown, and hurried downstairs trembling. There was nobody in the sitting-room; the piano was silent. She ran to Mrs. Dent's bedroom and called hysterically:

"Emeline! Emeline!"

"What is it?" asked Mrs. Dent's voice from the bed. The voice was stern, but had a note of consciousness in it.

"Who—who was that playing 'The Maiden's Prayer' in the sitting-room, on the piano?"

"I didn't hear anybody."

"There was some one."

"I didn't hear anything."

"I tell you there was some one. But—THERE AIN'T ANYBODY THERE."

"I didn't hear anything."

"I did—somebody playing 'The Maiden's Prayer' on the piano. Has Agnes got home? I WANT TO KNOW."

"Of course Agnes hasn't got home," answered Mrs. Dent with rising inflection. "Be you gone crazy over that girl? The last boat from Porter's Falls was in before we went to bed. Of course she ain't come."

"I heard—"

"You were dreaming."

"I wasn't; I was broad awake."

Rebecca went back to her chamber and kept her lamp burning all night.

The next morning her eyes upon Mrs. Dent were wary and blazing with suppressed excitement. She kept opening her mouth as if to speak, then frowning, and setting her lips hard. After breakfast she went upstairs, and came down presently with her coat and bonnet.

"Now, Emeline," she said, "I want to know where the Slocums live."

Mrs. Dent gave a strange, long, half-lidded glance at her. She was finishing her coffee.

"Why?" she asked.

"I'm going over there and find out if they have heard anything from her daughter and Agnes since they went away. I don't like what I heard last night."

"You must have been dreaming."

"It don't make any odds whether I was or not. Does she play 'The Maiden's Prayer' on the piano? I want to know."

"What if she does? She plays it a little, I believe. I don't know. She don't half play it, anyhow; she ain't got an ear."

"That wasn't half played last night. I don't like such things happening. I ain't superstitious, but I don't like it. I'm going. Where do the Slocums live?"

"You go down the road over the bridge past the old grist mill, then you turn to the left; it's the only house for half a mile. You can't miss it. It has a barn with a ship in full sail on the cupola."

"Well, I'm going. I don't feel easy."

About two hours later Rebecca returned. There were red spots on her cheeks. She looked wild. "I've been there," she said, "and there isn't a soul at home. Something HAS happened."

"What has happened?"

"I don't know. Something. I had a warning last night. There wasn't a soul there. They've been sent for to Lincoln."

"Did you see anybody to ask?" asked Mrs. Dent with thinly concealed anxiety.

"I asked the woman that lives on the turn of the road. She's stone deaf. I suppose you know. She listened while I screamed at her to know where the Slocums were, and then she said, 'Mrs. Smith don't live here.' I didn't see anybody on the road, and that's the only house. What do you suppose it means?"

"I don't suppose it means much of anything," replied Mrs. Dent coolly. "Mr. Slocum is conductor on the railroad, and he'd be away anyway, and Mrs. Slocum often goes early when he does, to spend the day with her sister in Porter's Falls. She'd be more likely to go away than Addie."

"And you don't think anything has happened?" Rebecca asked with diminishing distrust before the reasonableness of it.

"Land, no!"

Rebecca went upstairs to lay aside her coat and bonnet. But she came hurrying back with them still on.

"Who's been in my room?" she gasped. Her face was pale as ashes.

Mrs. Dent also paled as she regarded her.

"What do you mean?" she asked slowly.

"I found when I went upstairs that—little nightgown of— Agnes's on—the bed, laid out. It was—LAID OUT. The sleeves were folded across the bosom, and there was that little red rose between them. Emeline, what is it? Emeline, what's the matter? Oh!"

Mrs. Dent was struggling for breath in great, choking gasps. She clung to the back of a chair. Rebecca, trembling herself so she could scarcely keep on her feet, got her some water.

As soon as she recovered herself Mrs. Dent regarded her with eyes full of the strangest mixture of fear and horror and hostility.

"What do you mean talking so?" she said in a hard voice.

"It IS THERE."

"Nonsense. You threw it down and it fell that way."

"It was folded in my bureau drawer."

"It couldn't have been."

"Who picked that red rose?"

"Look on the bush," Mrs. Dent replied shortly.

Rebecca looked at her; her mouth gaped. She hurried out of the room. When she came back her eyes seemed to protrude. (She had in the meantime hastened upstairs, and come down with tottering steps, clinging to the banisters.)

"Now I want to know what all this means?" she demanded.

"What what means?"

"The rose is on the bush, and it's gone from the bed in my room! Is this house haunted, or what?"

"I don't know anything about a house being haunted. I don't believe in such things. Be you crazy?" Mrs. Dent spoke with gathering force. The colour flashed back to her cheeks.

"No," said Rebecca shortly. "I ain't crazy yet, but I shall be if this keeps on much longer. I'm going to find out where that girl is before night."

Mrs. Dent eyed her.

"What be you going to do?"

"I'm going to Lincoln."

A faint triumphant smile overspread Mrs. Dent's large face.

"You can't," said she; "there ain't any train."

"No train?"

"No; there ain't any afternoon train from the Falls to Lincoln."

"Then I'm going over to the Slocums' again tonight."

However, Rebecca did not go; such a rain came up as deterred even her resolution, and she had only her best dresses with her. Then in the evening came the letter from the Michigan village which she had left nearly a week ago. It was from her cousin, a single woman, who had come to keep her house while she was away. It was a pleasant unexciting letter enough, all the first of it, and related mostly how she missed Rebecca; how she hoped she was having pleasant weather and kept her health; and how her friend, Mrs. Greenaway, had come to stay with her since she had felt lonesome the first night in the house; how she hoped Rebecca would have no objections to this, although nothing had been said about it, since she had not realized that she might be nervous alone. The cousin was painfully conscientious, hence the letter. Rebecca smiled in spite of her disturbed mind as she read it, then her eye caught the postscript. That was in a different hand, purporting to be written by the friend, Mrs. Hannah Greenaway, informing her that the cousin had fallen down the cellar stairs and broken her hip, and was in a dangerous condition, and begging Rebecca to return at once, as she herself was rheumatic and unable to nurse her properly, and no one else could be obtained.

Rebecca looked at Mrs. Dent, who had come to her room with the letter quite late; it was half-past nine, and she had gone upstairs for the night.

"Where did this come from?" she asked.

"Mr. Amblecrom brought it," she replied.

"Who's he?"

"The postmaster. He often brings the letters that come on the late mail. He knows I ain't anybody to send. He brought yours about your coming. He said he and his wife came over on the ferry-boat with you."

"I remember him," Rebecca replied shortly. "There's bad news in this letter."

Mrs. Dent's face took on an expression of serious inquiry.

"Yes, my Cousin Harriet has fallen down the cellar stairs— they were always dangerous—and she's broken her hip, and I've got to take the first train home tomorrow."

"You don't say so. I'm dreadfully sorry."

"No, you ain't sorry!" said Rebecca, with a look as if she leaped. "You're glad. I don't know why, but you're glad. You've wanted to get rid of me for some reason ever since I came. I don't know why. You're a strange woman. Now you've got your way, and I hope you're satisfied."

"How you talk."

Mrs. Dent spoke in a faintly injured voice, but there was a light in her eyes.

"I talk the way it is. Well, I'm going tomorrow morning, and I want you, just as soon as Agnes Dent comes home, to send her out to me. Don't you wait for anything. You pack what clothes she's got, and don't wait even to mend them, and you buy her ticket. I'll leave the money, and you send her along. She don't have to change cars. You start her off, when she gets home, on the next train!"

"Very well," replied the other woman. She had an expression of covert amusement.

"Mind you do it."

"Very well, Rebecca."

Rebecca started on her journey the next morning. When she arrived, two days later, she found her cousin in perfect health. She found, moreover, that the friend had not written the postscript in the cousin's letter. Rebecca would have returned to Ford Village the next morning, but the fatigue and nervous strain had been too much for her. She was not able to move from her bed. She had a species of low fever induced by anxiety and fatigue. But she could write, and she did, to the Slocums, and she received no answer. She also wrote to Mrs. Dent; she even sent numerous telegrams, with no response. Finally she wrote to the postmaster, and an answer arrived by the first possible mail. The letter was short, curt, and to the purpose. Mr. Amblecrom, the postmaster, was a man of few words, and especially wary as to his expressions in a letter.

"Dear madam," he wrote, "your favour rec'ed. No Slocums in Ford's Village. All dead. Addie ten years ago, her mother two years later, her father five. House vacant. Mrs. John Dent said to have neglected stepdaughter. Girl was sick. Medicine not given. Talk of taking action. Not enough evidence. House said to be haunted. Strange sights and sounds. Your niece, Agnes Dent, died a year ago, about this time.

"Yours truly,

"THOMAS AMBLECROM."

THE SHADOWS ON THE WALL

"Henry had words with Edward in the study the night before Edward died," said Caroline Glynn.

She was elderly, tall, and harshly thin, with a hard colourlessness of face. She spoke not with acrimony, but with grave severity. Rebecca Ann Glynn, younger, stouter and rosy of face between her crinkling puffs of gray hair, gasped, by way of assent. She sat in a wide flounce of black silk in the corner of the sofa, and rolled terrified eyes from her sister Caroline to her sister Mrs. Stephen Brigham, who had been Emma Glynn, the one beauty of the family. She was beautiful still, with a large, splendid, full-blown beauty; she filled a great rocking-chair with her superb bulk of femininity, and swayed gently back and forth, her black silks whispering and her black frills fluttering. Even the shock of death (for her brother Edward lay dead in the house,) could not disturb her outward serenity of demeanour. She was grieved over the loss of her brother: he had been the youngest, and she had been fond of him, but never had Emma Brigham lost sight of her own importance amidst the waters of tribulation. She was always awake to the consciousness of her own stability in the midst of vicissitudes and the splendour of her permanent bearing.

But even her expression of masterly placidity changed before her sister Caroline's announcement and her sister Rebecca Ann's gasp of terror and distress in response.

"I think Henry might have controlled his temper, when poor Edward was so near his end," said she with an asperity which disturbed slightly the roseate curves of her beautiful mouth.

"Of course he did not KNOW," murmured Rebecca Ann in a faint tone strangely out of keeping with her appearance.

One involuntarily looked again to be sure that such a feeble pipe came from that full-swelling chest.

"Of course he did not know it," said Caroline quickly. She turned on her sister with a strange sharp look of suspicion. "How could he have known it?" said she. Then she shrank as if from the other's possible answer. "Of course you and I both know he could not," said she conclusively, but her pale face was paler than it had been before.

Rebecca gasped again. The married sister, Mrs. Emma Brigham, was now sitting up straight in her chair; she had ceased rocking, and was eyeing them both intently with a sudden accentuation of family likeness in her face. Given one common intensity of emotion and similar lines showed forth, and the three sisters of one race were evident.

"What do you mean?" said she impartially to them both. Then she, too, seemed to shrink before a possible answer. She even laughed an evasive sort of laugh. "I guess you don't mean anything," said she, but her face wore still the expression of shrinking horror.

"Nobody means anything," said Caroline firmly. She rose and crossed the room toward the door with grim decisiveness.

"Where are you going?" asked Mrs. Brigham.

"I have something to see to," replied Caroline, and the others at once knew by her tone that she had some solemn and sad duty to perform in the chamber of death.

"Oh," said Mrs. Brigham.

After the door had closed behind Caroline, she turned to Rebecca.

"Did Henry have many words with him?" she asked.

"They were talking very loud," replied Rebecca evasively, yet with an answering gleam of ready response to the other's curiosity in the quick lift of her soft blue eyes.

Mrs. Brigham looked at her. She had not resumed rocking. She still sat up straight with a slight knitting of intensity on her fair forehead, between the pretty rippling curves of her auburn hair.

"Did you—hear anything?" she asked in a low voice with a glance toward the door.

"I was just across the hall in the south parlour, and that door was open and this door ajar," replied Rebecca with a slight flush.

"Then you must have—"

"I couldn't help it."

"Everything?"

"Most of it."

"What was it?"

"The old story."

"I suppose Henry was mad, as he always was, because Edward was living on here for nothing, when he had wasted all the money father left him."

Rebecca nodded with a fearful glance at the door.

When Emma spoke again her voice was still more hushed. "I know how he felt," said she. "He had always been so prudent himself, and worked hard at his profession, and there Edward had never done anything but spend, and it must have looked to him as if Edward was living at his expense, but he wasn't."

"No, he wasn't."

"It was the way father left the property—that all the children should have a home here—and he left money enough to buy the food and all if we had all come home."

"Yes."

"And Edward had a right here according to the terms of father's will, and Henry ought to have remembered it."

"Yes, he ought."

"Did he say hard things?"

"Pretty hard from what I heard."

"What?"

"I heard him tell Edward that he had no business here at all, and he thought he had better go away."

"What did Edward say?"

"That he would stay here as long as he lived and afterward, too, if he was a mind to, and he would like to see Henry get him out; and then—"

"What?"

"Then he laughed."

"What did Henry say."

"I didn't hear him say anything, but—"

"But what?"

"I saw him when he came out of this room."

"He looked mad?"

"You've seen him when he looked so."

Emma nodded; the expression of horror on her face had deepened.

"Do you remember that time he killed the cat because she had scratched him?"

"Yes. Don't!"

Then Caroline reentered the room. She went up to the stove in which a wood fire was burning—it was a cold, gloomy day of fall—and she warmed her hands, which were reddened from recent washing in cold water.

Mrs. Brigham looked at her and hesitated. She glanced at the door, which was still ajar, as it did not easily shut, being still swollen with the damp weather of the summer. She rose and pushed it together with a sharp thud which jarred the house. Rebecca started painfully with a half exclamation. Caroline looked at her disapprovingly.

"It is time you controlled your nerves, Rebecca," said she.

"I can't help it," replied Rebecca with almost a wail. "I am nervous. There's enough to make me so, the Lord knows."

"What do you mean by that?" asked Caroline with her old air of sharp suspicion, and something between challenge and dread of its being met.

Rebecca shrank.

"Nothing," said she.

"Then I wouldn't keep speaking in such a fashion."

Emma, returning from the closed door, said imperiously that it ought to be fixed, it shut so hard.

"It will shrink enough after we have had the fire a few days," replied Caroline. "If anything is done to it it will be too small; there will be a crack at the sill."

"I think Henry ought to be ashamed of himself for talking as he did to Edward," said Mrs. Brigham abruptly, but in an almost inaudible voice.

"Hush!" said Caroline, with a glance of actual fear at the closed door.

"Nobody can hear with the door shut."

"He must have heard it shut, and—"

"Well, I can say what I want to before he comes down, and I am not afraid of him."

"I don't know who is afraid of him! What reason is there for anybody to be afraid of Henry?" demanded Caroline.

Mrs. Brigham trembled before her sister's look. Rebecca gasped again. "There isn't any reason, of course. Why should there be?"

"I wouldn't speak so, then. Somebody might overhear you and think it was queer. Miranda Joy is in the south parlour sewing, you know."

"I thought she went upstairs to stitch on the machine."

"She did, but she has come down again."

"Well, she can't hear."

"I say again I think Henry ought to be ashamed of himself. I shouldn't think he'd ever get over it, having words with poor Edward the very night before he died. Edward was enough sight better disposition than Henry, with all his faults. I always thought a great deal of poor Edward, myself."

Mrs. Brigham passed a large fluff of handkerchief across her eyes; Rebecca sobbed outright.

"Rebecca," said Caroline admonishingly, keeping her mouth stiff and swallowing determinately.

"I never heard him speak a cross word, unless he spoke cross to Henry that last night. I don't know, but he did from what Rebecca overheard," said Emma.

"Not so much cross as sort of soft, and sweet, and aggravating," sniffled Rebecca.

"He never raised his voice," said Caroline; "but he had his way."

"He had a right to in this case."

"Yes, he did."

"He had as much of a right here as Henry," sobbed Rebecca, "and now he's gone, and he will never be in this home that poor father left him and the rest of us again."

"What do you really think ailed Edward?" asked Emma in hardly more than a whisper. She did not look at her sister.

Caroline sat down in a nearby armchair, and clutched the arms convulsively until her thin knuckles whitened.

"I told you," said she.

Rebecca held her handkerchief over her mouth, and looked at them above it with terrified, streaming eyes.

"I know you said that he had terrible pains in his stomach, and had spasms, but what do you think made him have them?"

"Henry called it gastric trouble. You know Edward has always had dyspepsia."

Mrs. Brigham hesitated a moment. "Was there any talk of an—examination?" said she.

Then Caroline turned on her fiercely.

"No," said she in a terrible voice. "No."

The three sisters' souls seemed to meet on one common ground of terrified understanding though their eyes. The old-fashioned latch of the door was heard to rattle, and a push from without made the door shake ineffectually. "It's Henry," Rebecca sighed rather than whispered. Mrs. Brigham settled herself after a noiseless rush across the floor into her rocking-chair again, and was swaying back and forth with her head comfortably leaning back, when the door at last yielded and Henry Glynn entered. He cast a covertly sharp, comprehensive glance at Mrs. Brigham with her elaborate calm; at Rebecca quietly huddled in the corner of the sofa with her handkerchief to her face and only one small reddened ear as attentive as a dog's uncovered and revealing her alertness for his presence; at Caroline sitting with a strained composure in her armchair by the stove. She met his eyes quite firmly with a look of inscrutable fear, and defiance of the fear and of him.

Henry Glynn looked more like this sister than the others. Both had the same hard delicacy of form and feature, both were tall and almost emaciated, both had a sparse growth of gray blond hair far back from high intellectual foreheads, both had an almost noble aquilinity of feature. They confronted each other with the pitiless immovability of two statues in whose marble lineaments emotions were fixed for all eternity.

Then Henry Glynn smiled and the smile transformed his face. He looked suddenly years younger, and an almost boyish recklessness and irresolution appeared in his face. He flung himself into a chair with a gesture which was bewildering from its incongruity with his general appearance. He leaned his head back, flung one leg over the other, and looked laughingly at Mrs. Brigham.

"I declare, Emma, you grow younger every year," he said.

She flushed a little, and her placid mouth widened at the corners. She was susceptible to praise.

"Our thoughts today ought to belong to the one of us who will NEVER grow older," said Caroline in a hard voice.

Henry looked at her, still smiling. "Of course, we none of us forget that," said he, in a deep, gentle voice, "but we have to speak to the living, Caroline, and I have not seen Emma for a long time, and the living are as dear as the dead."

"Not to me," said Caroline.

She rose, and went abruptly out of the room again. Rebecca also rose and hurried after her, sobbing loudly.

Henry looked slowly after them.

"Caroline is completely unstrung," said he. Mrs. Brigham rocked. A confidence in him inspired by his manner was stealing over her. Out of that confidence she spoke quite easily and naturally.

"His death was very sudden," said she.

Henry's eyelids quivered slightly but his gaze was unswerving.

"Yes," said he; "it was very sudden. He was sick only a few hours."

"What did you call it?"

"Gastric."

"You did not think of an examination?"

"There was no need. I am perfectly certain as to the cause of his death."

Suddenly Mrs. Brigham felt a creep as of some live horror over her very soul. Her flesh prickled with cold, before an inflection of his voice. She rose, tottering on weak knees.

"Where are you going?" asked Henry in a strange, breathless voice.

Mrs. Brigham said something incoherent about some sewing which she had to do, some black for the funeral, and was out of the room. She went up to the front chamber which she occupied. Caroline was there. She went close to her and took her hands, and the two sisters looked at each other.

"Don't speak, don't, I won't have it!" said Caroline finally in an awful whisper.

"I won't," replied Emma.

That afternoon the three sisters were in the study, the large front room on the ground floor across the hall from the south parlour, when the dusk deepened.

Mrs. Brigham was hemming some black material. She sat close to the west window for the waning light. At last she laid her work on her lap.

"It's no use, I cannot see to sew another stitch until we have a light," said she.

Caroline, who was writing some letters at the table, turned to Rebecca, in her usual place on the sofa.

"Rebecca, you had better get a lamp," she said.

Rebecca started up; even in the dusk her face showed her agitation.

"It doesn't seem to me that we need a lamp quite yet," she said in a piteous, pleading voice like a child's.

"Yes, we do," returned Mrs. Brigham peremptorily. "We must have a light. I must finish this tonight or I can't go to the funeral, and I can't see to sew another stitch."

"Caroline can see to write letters, and she is farther from the window than you are," said Rebecca.

"Are you trying to save kerosene or are you lazy, Rebecca Glynn?" cried Mrs. Brigham. "I can go and get the light myself, but I have this work all in my lap."

Caroline's pen stopped scratching.

"Rebecca, we must have the light," said she.

"Had we better have it in here?" asked Rebecca weakly.

"Of course! Why not?" cried Caroline sternly.

"I am sure I don't want to take my sewing into the other room, when it is all cleaned up for tomorrow," said Mrs. Brigham.

"Why, I never heard such a to-do about lighting a lamp."

Rebecca rose and left the room. Presently she entered with a lamp—a large one with a white porcelain shade. She set it on a table, an old-fashioned card-table which was placed against the opposite wall from the window. That wall was clear of bookcases and books, which were only on three sides of the room. That opposite wall was taken up with three doors, the one small space being occupied by the table. Above the table on the old-fashioned paper, of a white satin gloss, traversed by an indeterminate green scroll, hung quite high a small gilt and black-framed ivory miniature taken in her girlhood of the mother of the family. When the lamp was set on the table beneath it, the tiny pretty face painted on the ivory seemed to gleam out with a look of intelligence.

"What have you put that lamp over there for?" asked Mrs. Brigham, with more of impatience than her voice usually revealed. "Why didn't you set it in the hall and have done with it. Neither Caroline nor I can see if it is on that table."

"I thought perhaps you would move," replied Rebecca hoarsely.

"If I do move, we can't both sit at that table. Caroline has her paper all spread around. Why don't you set the lamp on the study table in the middle of the room, then we can both see?"

Rebecca hesitated. Her face was very pale. She looked with an appeal that was fairly agonizing at her sister Caroline.

"Why don't you put the lamp on this table, as she says?" asked Caroline, almost fiercely. "Why do you act so, Rebecca?"

"I should think you WOULD ask her that," said Mrs. Brigham. "She doesn't act like herself at all."

Rebecca took the lamp and set it on the table in the middle of the room without another word. Then she turned her back upon it quickly and seated herself on the sofa, and placed a hand over her eyes as if to shade them, and remained so.

"Does the light hurt your eyes, and is that the reason why you didn't want the lamp?" asked Mrs. Brigham kindly.

"I always like to sit in the dark," replied Rebecca chokingly. Then she snatched her handkerchief hastily from her pocket and began to weep. Caroline continued to write, Mrs. Brigham to sew.

Suddenly Mrs. Brigham as she sewed glanced at the opposite wall. The glance became a steady stare. She looked intently, her work suspended in her hands. Then she looked away again and took a few more stitches, then she looked again, and again turned to her task. At last she laid her work in her lap and stared concentratedly. She looked from the wall around the room, taking note of the various objects; she looked at the wall long and intently. Then she turned to her sisters.

"What IS that?" said she.

"What?" asked Caroline harshly; her pen scratched loudly across the paper.

Rebecca gave one of her convulsive gasps.

"That strange shadow on the wall," replied Mrs. Brigham.

Rebecca sat with her face hidden: Caroline dipped her pen in the inkstand.

"Why don't you turn around and look?" asked Mrs. Brigham in a wondering and somewhat aggrieved way.

"I am in a hurry to finish this letter, if Mrs. Wilson Ebbit is going to get word in time to come to the funeral," replied Caroline shortly.

Mrs. Brigham rose, her work slipping to the floor, and she began walking around the room, moving various articles of furniture, with her eyes on the shadow.

Then suddenly she shrieked out:

"Look at this awful shadow! What is it? Caroline, look, look! Rebecca, look! WHAT IS IT?"

All Mrs. Brigham's triumphant placidity was gone. Her handsome face was livid with horror. She stood stiffly pointing at the shadow.

"Look!" said she, pointing her finger at it. "Look! What is it?"

Then Rebecca burst out in a wild wail after a shuddering glance at the wall:

"Oh, Caroline, there it is again! There it is again!"

"Caroline Glynn, you look!" said Mrs. Brigham. "Look! What is that dreadful shadow?"

Caroline rose, turned, and stood confronting the wall.

"How should I know?" she said.

"It has been there every night since he died," cried Rebecca.

"Every night?"

"Yes. He died Thursday and this is Saturday; that makes three nights," said Caroline rigidly. She stood as if holding herself calm with a vise of concentrated will.

"It—it looks like—like—" stammered Mrs. Brigham in a tone of intense horror.

"I know what it looks like well enough," said Caroline. "I've got eyes in my head."

"It looks like Edward," burst out Rebecca in a sort of frenzy of fear. "Only—"

"Yes, it does," assented Mrs. Brigham, whose horror-stricken tone matched her sister's, "only—Oh, it is awful! What is it, Caroline?"

"I ask you again, how should I know?" replied Caroline. "I see it there like you. How should I know any more than you?"

"It MUST be something in the room," said Mrs. Brigham, staring wildly around.

"We moved everything in the room the first night it came," said Rebecca; "it is not anything in the room."

Caroline turned upon her with a sort of fury. "Of course it is something in the room," said she. "How you act! What do you mean by talking so? Of course it is something in the room."

"Of course, it is," agreed Mrs. Brigham, looking at Caroline suspiciously. "Of course it must be. It is only a coincidence. It just happens so. Perhaps it is that fold of the window curtain that makes it. It must be something in the room."

"It is not anything in the room," repeated Rebecca with obstinate horror.

The door opened suddenly and Henry Glynn entered. He began to speak, then his eyes followed the direction of the others'. He stood stock still staring at the shadow on the wall. It was life size and stretched across the white parallelogram of a door, half across the wall space on which the picture hung.

"What is that?" he demanded in a strange voice.

"It must be due to something in the room," Mrs. Brigham said faintly.

"It is not due to anything in the room," said Rebecca again with the shrill insistency of terror.

"How you act, Rebecca Glynn," said Caroline.

Henry Glynn stood and stared a moment longer. His face showed a gamut of emotions—horror, conviction, then furious incredulity. Suddenly he began hastening hither and thither about the room. He moved the furniture with fierce jerks, turning ever to see the effect upon the shadow on the wall. Not a line of its terrible outlines wavered.

"It must be something in the room!" he declared in a voice which seemed to snap like a lash.

His face changed. The inmost secrecy of his nature seemed evident until one almost lost sight of his lineaments. Rebecca stood close to her sofa, regarding him with woeful, fascinated eyes. Mrs. Brigham clutched Caroline's hand. They both stood in a corner out of his way. For a few moments he raged about the room like a caged wild animal. He moved every piece of furniture; when the moving of a piece did not affect the shadow, he flung it to the floor, the sisters watching.

Then suddenly he desisted. He laughed and began straightening the furniture which he had flung down.

"What an absurdity," he said easily. "Such a to-do about a shadow."

"That's so," assented Mrs. Brigham, in a scared voice which she tried to make natural. As she spoke she lifted a chair near her.

"I think you have broken the chair that Edward was so fond of," said Caroline.

Terror and wrath were struggling for expression on her face. Her mouth was set, her eyes shrinking. Henry lifted the chair with a show of anxiety.

"Just as good as ever," he said pleasantly. He laughed again, looking at his sisters. "Did I scare you?" he said. "I should think you might be used to me by this time. You know my way of wanting to leap to the bottom of a mystery, and that shadow does look— queer, like—and I thought if there was any way of accounting for it I would like to without any delay."

"You don't seem to have succeeded," remarked Caroline dryly, with a slight glance at the wall.

Henry's eyes followed hers and he quivered perceptibly.

"Oh, there is no accounting for shadows," he said, and he laughed again. "A man is a fool to try to account for shadows."

Then the supper bell rang, and they all left the room, but Henry kept his back to the wall, as did, indeed, the others.

Mrs. Brigham pressed close to Caroline as she crossed the hall. "He looked like a demon!" she breathed in her ear.

Henry led the way with an alert motion like a boy; Rebecca brought up the rear; she could scarcely walk, her knees trembled so.

"I can't sit in that room again this evening," she whispered to Caroline after supper.

"Very well, we will sit in the south room," replied Caroline. "I think we will sit in the south parlour," she said aloud; "it isn't as damp as the study, and I have a cold."

So they all sat in the south room with their sewing. Henry read the newspaper, his chair drawn close to the lamp on the table. About nine o'clock he rose abruptly and crossed the hall to the study. The three sisters looked at one another. Mrs. Brigham rose, folded her rustling skirts compactly around her, and began tiptoeing toward the door.

"What are you going to do?" inquired Rebecca agitatedly.

"I am going to see what he is about," replied Mrs. Brigham cautiously.

She pointed as she spoke to the study door across the hall; it was ajar. Henry had striven to pull it together behind him, but it had somehow swollen beyond the limit with curious speed. It was still ajar and a streak of light showed from top to bottom. The hall lamp was not lit.

"You had better stay where you are," said Caroline with guarded sharpness.

"I am going to see," repeated Mrs. Brigham firmly.

Then she folded her skirts so tightly that her bulk with its swelling curves was revealed in a black silk sheath, and she went with a slow toddle across the hall to the study door. She stood there, her eye at the crack.

In the south room Rebecca stopped sewing and sat watching with dilated eyes. Caroline sewed steadily. What Mrs. Brigham, standing at the crack in the study door, saw was this:

Henry Glynn, evidently reasoning that the source of the strange shadow must be between the table on which the lamp stood and the wall, was making systematic passes and thrusts all over and through the intervening space with an old sword which had belonged to his father. Not an inch was left unpierced. He seemed to have divided the space into mathematical sections. He brandished the sword with a sort of cold fury and calculation; the blade gave out flashes of light, the shadow remained unmoved. Mrs. Brigham, watching, felt herself cold with horror.

Finally Henry ceased and stood with the sword in hand and raised as if to strike, surveying the shadow on the wall threateningly. Mrs. Brigham toddled back across the hall and shut the south room door behind her before she related what she had seen.

"He looked like a demon!" she said again. "Have you got any of that old wine in the house, Caroline? I don't feel as if I could stand much more."

Indeed, she looked overcome. Her handsome placid face was worn and strained and pale.

"Yes, there's plenty," said Caroline; "you can have some when you go to bed."

"I think we had all better take some," said Mrs. Brigham. "Oh, my God, Caroline, what—"

"Don't ask and don't speak," said Caroline.

"No, I am not going to," replied Mrs. Brigham; "but—"

Rebecca moaned aloud.

"What are you doing that for?" asked Caroline harshly.

"Poor Edward," returned Rebecca.

"That is all you have to groan for," said Caroline. "There is nothing else."

"I am going to bed," said Mrs. Brigham. "I sha'n't be able to be at the funeral if I don't."

Soon the three sisters went to their chambers and the south parlour was deserted. Caroline called to Henry in the study to put out the light before he came upstairs. They had been gone about an hour when he came into the room bringing the lamp which had stood in the study. He set it on the table and waited a few minutes, pacing up and down. His face was terrible, his fair complexion showed livid; his blue eyes seemed dark blanks of awful reflections.

Then he took the lamp up and returned to the library. He set the lamp on the centre table, and the shadow sprang out on the wall. Again he studied the furniture and moved it about, but deliberately, with none of his former frenzy. Nothing affected the shadow. Then he returned to the south room with the lamp and again waited. Again he returned to the study and placed the lamp on the table, and the shadow sprang out upon the wall. It was midnight before he went upstairs. Mrs. Brigham and the other sisters, who could not sleep, heard him.

The next day was the funeral. That evening the family sat in the south room. Some relatives were with them. Nobody entered the study until Henry carried a lamp in there after the others had retired for the night. He saw again the shadow on the wall leap to an awful life before the light.

The next morning at breakfast Henry Glynn announced that he had to go to the city for three days. The sisters looked at him with surprise. He very seldom left home, and just now his practice had been neglected on account of Edward's death. He was a physician.

"How can you leave your patients now?" asked Mrs. Brigham wonderingly.

"I don't know how to, but there is no other way," replied Henry easily. "I have had a telegram from Doctor Mitford."

"Consultation?" inquired Mrs. Brigham.

"I have business," replied Henry.

Doctor Mitford was an old classmate of his who lived in a neighbouring city and who occasionally called upon him in the case of a consultation.

After he had gone Mrs. Brigham said to Caroline that after all Henry had not said that he was going to consult with Doctor Mitford, and she thought it very strange.

"Everything is very strange," said Rebecca with a shudder.

"What do you mean?" inquired Caroline sharply.

"Nothing," replied Rebecca.

Nobody entered the library that day, nor the next, nor the next. The third day Henry was expected home, but he did not arrive and the last train from the city had come.

"I call it pretty queer work," said Mrs. Brigham. "The idea of a doctor leaving his patients for three days anyhow, at such a time as this, and I know he has some very sick ones; he said so. And the idea of a consultation lasting three days! There is no sense in it, and NOW he has not come. I don't understand it, for my part."

"I don't either," said Rebecca.

They were all in the south parlour. There was no light in the study opposite, and the door was ajar.

Presently Mrs. Brigham rose—she could not have told why; something seemed to impel her, some will outside her own. She went out of the room, again wrapping her rustling skirts around that she might pass noiselessly, and began pushing at the swollen door of the study.

"She has not got any lamp," said Rebecca in a shaking voice.

Caroline, who was writing letters, rose again, took a lamp (there were two in the room) and followed her sister. Rebecca had risen, but she stood trembling, not venturing to follow.

The doorbell rang, but the others did not hear it; it was on the south door on the other side of the house from the study. Rebecca, after hesitating until the bell rang the second time, went to the door; she remembered that the servant was out.

Caroline and her sister Emma entered the study. Caroline set the lamp on the table. They looked at the wall. "Oh, my God," gasped Mrs. Brigham, "there are—there are TWO—shadows." The sisters stood clutching each other, staring at the awful things on the wall. Then Rebecca came in, staggering, with a telegram in her hand. "Here is—a telegram," she gasped. "Henry is—dead."

LUELLA MILLER

Close to the village street stood the one-story house in which Luella Miller, who had an evil name in the village, had dwelt. She had been dead for years, yet there were those in the village who, in spite of the clearer light which comes on a vantage-point from a long-past danger, half believed in the tale which they had heard from their childhood. In their hearts, although they scarcely would have owned it, was a survival of the wild horror and frenzied fear of their ancestors who had dwelt in the same age with Luella Miller. Young people even would stare with a shudder at the old house as they passed, and children never played around it as was their wont around an untenanted building. Not a window in the old Miller house was broken: the panes reflected the morning sunlight in patches of emerald and blue, and the latch of the sagging front door was never lifted, although no bolt secured it. Since Luella Miller had been carried out of it, the house had had no tenant except one friendless old soul who had no choice between that and the far-off shelter of the open sky. This old woman, who had survived her kindred and friends, lived in the house one week, then one morning no smoke came out of the chimney, and a body of neighbours, a score strong, entered and found her dead in her bed. There were dark whispers as to the cause of her death, and there were those who testified to an expression of fear so exalted that it showed forth the state of the departing soul upon the dead face. The old woman had been hale and hearty when she entered the house, and in seven days she was dead; it seemed that she had fallen a victim to some uncanny power. The minister talked in the pulpit with covert severity against the sin of superstition; still the belief prevailed. Not a soul in the village but would have chosen the almshouse rather than that dwelling. No vagrant, if he heard the tale, would seek shelter beneath that old roof, unhallowed by nearly half a century of superstitious fear.

There was only one person in the village who had actually known Luella Miller. That person was a woman well over eighty, but a marvel of vitality and unextinct youth. Straight as an arrow, with the spring of one recently let loose from the bow of life, she moved about the streets, and she always went to church, rain or shine. She had never married, and had lived alone for years in a house across the road from Luella Miller's.

This woman had none of the garrulousness of age, but never in all her life had she ever held her tongue for any will save her own, and she never spared the truth when she essayed to present it. She it was who bore testimony to the life, evil, though possibly wittingly or designedly so, of Luella Miller, and to her personal appearance. When this old woman spoke—and she had the gift of description, although her thoughts were clothed in the rude vernacular of her native village—one could seem to see Luella Miller as she had really looked. According to this woman, Lydia Anderson by name, Luella Miller had been a beauty of a type rather unusual in New England. She had been a slight, pliant sort of creature, as ready with a strong yielding to fate and as unbreakable as a willow. She had glimmering lengths of straight, fair hair, which she wore softly looped round a long, lovely face. She had blue eyes full of soft pleading, little slender, clinging hands, and a wonderful grace of motion and attitude.

"Luella Miller used to sit in a way nobody else could if they sat up and studied a week of Sundays," said Lydia Anderson, "and it was a sight to see her walk. If one of them willows over there on the edge of the brook could start up and get its roots free of the ground, and move off, it would go just the way Luella Miller used to. She had a green shot silk she used to wear, too, and a hat with green ribbon streamers, and a lace veil blowing across her face and out sideways, and a green ribbon flyin' from her waist. That was what she came out bride in when she married Erastus Miller. Her name before she was married was Hill. There was always a sight of "l's" in her name, married or single. Erastus Miller was good lookin', too, better lookin' than Luella. Sometimes I used to think that Luella wa'n't so handsome after all. Erastus just about worshiped her. I used to know him pretty well. He lived next door to me, and we went to school together. Folks used to say he was waitin' on me, but he wa'n't. I never thought he was except once or twice when he said things that some girls might have suspected meant somethin'. That was before Luella came here to teach the district school. It was funny how she came to get it, for folks said she hadn't any education, and that one of the big girls, Lottie Henderson, used to do all the teachin' for her, while she sat back and did embroidery work on a cambric pocket-handkerchief. Lottie Henderson was a real smart girl, a splendid scholar, and she just set her eyes by Luella, as all the girls did. Lottie would have made a real smart woman, but she died when Luella had been here about a year—just faded away and died: nobody knew what ailed her. She dragged herself to that schoolhouse and helped Luella teach till the very last minute. The committee all knew how Luella didn't do much of the work herself, but they winked at it. It wa'n't long after Lottie died that Erastus married her. I always thought he hurried it up because she wa'n't fit to teach. One of the big boys used to help her after Lottie died, but he hadn't much government, and the school didn't do very well, and Luella might have had to give it up, for the committee couldn't have shut their eyes to things much longer. The boy that helped her was a real honest, innocent sort of fellow, and he was a good scholar, too. Folks said he overstudied, and that was the reason he was took crazy the year after Luella married, but I don't know. And I don't know what made Erastus Miller go into consumption of the blood the year after he was married: consumption wa'n't in his family. He just grew weaker and weaker, and went almost bent double when he tried to wait on Luella, and he spoke feeble, like an old man. He worked terrible hard till the last trying to save up a little to leave Luella. I've seen him out in the worst storms on a wood-sled—he used to cut and sell wood—and he was hunched up on top lookin' more dead than alive. Once I couldn't stand it: I went over and helped him pitch some wood on the cart—I was always strong in my arms. I wouldn't stop for all he told me to, and I guess he was glad enough for the help. That was only a week before he died. He fell on the kitchen floor while he was gettin' breakfast. He always got the breakfast and let Luella lay abed. He did all the sweepin' and the washin' and the ironin' and most of the cookin'. He couldn't bear to have Luella lift her finger, and she let him do for her. She lived like a queen for all the work she did.

She didn't even do her sewin'. She said it made her shoulder ache to sew, and poor Erastus's sister Lily used to do all her sewin'. She wa'n't able to, either; she was never strong in her back, but she did it beautifully. She had to, to suit Luella, she was so dreadful particular. I never saw anythin' like the fagottin' and hemstitchin' that Lily Miller did for Luella. She made all Luella's weddin' outfit, and that green silk dress, after Maria Babbit cut it. Maria she cut it for nothin', and she did a lot more cuttin' and fittin' for nothin' for Luella, too. Lily Miller went to live with Luella after Erastus died. She gave up her home, though she was real attached to it and wa'n't a mite afraid to stay alone. She rented it and she went to live with Luella right away after the funeral."

Then this old woman, Lydia Anderson, who remembered Luella Miller, would go on to relate the story of Lily Miller. It seemed that on the removal of Lily Miller to the house of her dead brother, to live with his widow, the village people first began to talk. This Lily Miller had been hardly past her first youth, and a most robust and blooming woman, rosy-cheeked, with curls of strong, black hair overshadowing round, candid temples and bright dark eyes. It was not six months after she had taken up her residence with her sister-in-law that her rosy colour faded and her pretty curves became wan hollows. White shadows began to show in the black rings of her hair, and the light died out of her eyes, her features sharpened, and there were pathetic lines at her mouth, which yet wore always an expression of utter sweetness and even happiness. She was devoted to her sister; there was no doubt that she loved her with her whole heart, and was perfectly content in her service. It was her sole anxiety lest she should die and leave her alone.

"The way Lily Miller used to talk about Luella was enough to make you mad and enough to make you cry," said Lydia Anderson. "I've been in there sometimes toward the last when she was too feeble to cook and carried her some blanc-mange or custard— somethin' I thought she might relish, and she'd thank me, and when I asked her how she was, say she felt better than she did yesterday, and asked me if I didn't think she looked better, dreadful pitiful, and say poor Luella had an awful time takin' care of her and doin' the work—she wa'n't strong enough to do anythin'—when all the time Luella wa'n't liftin' her finger and poor Lily didn't get any care except what the neighbours gave her, and Luella eat up everythin' that was carried in for Lily. I had it real straight that she did. Luella used to just sit and cry and do nothin'. She did act real fond of Lily, and she pined away considerable, too. There was those that thought she'd go into a decline herself. But after Lily died, her Aunt Abby Mixter came, and then Luella picked up and grew as fat and rosy as ever. But poor Aunt Abby begun to droop just the way Lily had, and I guess somebody wrote to her married daughter, Mrs. Sam Abbot, who lived in Barre, for she wrote her mother that she must leave right away and come and make her a visit, but Aunt Abby wouldn't go. I can see her now. She was a real good-lookin' woman, tall and large, with a big, square face and a high forehead that looked of itself kind of benevolent and good. She just tended out on Luella as if she had been a baby, and when her married daughter sent for her she wouldn't stir one inch. She'd always thought a lot of her daughter, too, but she said Luella needed her and her married daughter didn't. Her daughter kept writin' and writin', but it didn't do any good. Finally she came, and when she saw how bad her mother looked, she broke down and cried and all but went on her knees to have her come away. She spoke her mind out to Luella, too. She told her that she'd killed her husband and everybody that had anythin' to do with her, and she'd thank her to leave her mother alone. Luella went into hysterics, and Aunt Abby was so frightened that she called me after her daughter went. Mrs. Sam Abbot she went away fairly cryin' out loud in the buggy, the neighbours heard her, and well she might, for she never saw her mother again alive. I went in that night when Aunt Abby called for me, standin' in the door with her little green-checked shawl over her head. I can see her now. 'Do come over here, Miss Anderson,' she sung out, kind of gasping for breath. I didn't stop for anythin'. I put over as fast as I could, and when I got there, there was Luella laughin' and cryin' all together, and Aunt Abby trying to hush her, and all the time she herself was white as a sheet and shakin' so she could hardly stand. 'For the land sakes, Mrs. Mixter,' says I, 'you look worse than she does. You ain't fit to be up out of your bed.'

"'Oh, there ain't anythin' the matter with me,' says she. Then she went on talkin' to Luella. 'There, there, don't, don't, poor little lamb,' says she. 'Aunt Abby is here. She ain't goin' away and leave you. Don't, poor little lamb.'

"'Do leave her with me, Mrs. Mixter, and you get back to bed,' says I, for Aunt Abby had been layin' down considerable lately, though somehow she contrived to do the work.

"'I'm well enough,' says she. 'Don't you think she had better have the doctor, Miss Anderson?'

"'The doctor,' says I, 'I think YOU had better have the doctor. I think you need him much worse than some folks I could mention.' And I looked right straight at Luella Miller laughin' and cryin' and goin' on as if she was the centre of all creation. All the time she was actin' so—seemed as if she was too sick to sense anythin'—she was keepin' a sharp lookout as to how we took it out of the corner of one eye. I see her. You could never cheat me about Luella Miller. Finally I got real mad and I run home and I got a bottle of valerian I had, and I poured some boilin' hot water on a handful of catnip, and I mixed up that catnip tea with most half a wineglass of valerian, and I went with it over to Luella's. I marched right up to Luella, a-holdin' out of that cup, all smokin'. 'Now,' says I, 'Luella Miller, 'YOU SWALLER THIS!'

"'What is—what is it, oh, what is it?' she sort of screeches out. Then she goes off a-laughin' enough to kill.

"'Poor lamb, poor little lamb,' says Aunt Abby, standin' over her, all kind of tottery, and tryin' to bathe her head with camphor.

"'YOU SWALLER THIS RIGHT DOWN,' says I. And I didn't waste any ceremony. I just took hold of Luella Miller's chin and I tipped her head back, and I caught her mouth open with laughin', and I clapped that cup to her lips, and I fairly hollered at her: 'Swaller, swaller, swaller!' and she gulped it right down. She had to, and I guess it did her good. Anyhow, she stopped cryin' and laughin' and let me put her to bed, and she went to sleep like a baby inside of half an hour. That was more than poor Aunt Abby did. She lay awake all that night and I stayed with her, though she tried not to have me; said she wa'n't sick enough for watchers. But I stayed, and I made some good cornmeal gruel and I fed her a teaspoon every little while all night long. It seemed to me as if she was jest dyin' from bein' all wore out. In the mornin' as soon as it was light I run over to the Bisbees and sent Johnny Bisbee for the doctor. I told him to tell the doctor to hurry, and he come pretty quick. Poor Aunt Abby didn't seem to know much of anythin' when he got there. You couldn't hardly tell she breathed, she was so used up. When the doctor had gone, Luella came into the room lookin' like a baby in her ruffled nightgown. I can see her now. Her eyes were as blue and her face all pink and white like a blossom, and she looked at Aunt Abby in the bed sort of innocent and surprised. 'Why,' says she, 'Aunt Abby ain't got up yet?'

"'No, she ain't,' says I, pretty short.

"'I thought I didn't smell the coffee,' says Luella.

"'Coffee,' says I. 'I guess if you have coffee this mornin' you'll make it yourself.'

"'I never made the coffee in all my life,' says she, dreadful astonished. 'Erastus always made the coffee as long as he lived, and then Lily she made it, and then Aunt Abby made it. I don't believe I CAN make the coffee, Miss Anderson.'

"'You can make it or go without, jest as you please,' says I.

"'Ain't Aunt Abby goin' to get up?' says she.

"'I guess she won't get up,' says I, 'sick as she is.' I was gettin' madder and madder. There was somethin' about that little pink-and-white thing standin' there and talkin' about coffee, when she had killed so many better folks than she was, and had jest killed another, that made me feel 'most as if I wished somebody would up and kill her before she had a chance to do any more harm.

"'Is Aunt Abby sick?' says Luella, as if she was sort of aggrieved and injured.

"'Yes,' says I, 'she's sick, and she's goin' to die, and then you'll be left alone, and you'll have to do for yourself and wait on yourself, or do without things.' I don't know but I was sort of hard, but it was the truth, and if I was any harder than Luella Miller had been I'll give up. I ain't never been sorry that I said it. Well, Luella, she up and had hysterics again at that, and I jest let her have 'em. All I did was to bundle her into the room on the other side of the entry where Aunt Abby couldn't hear her, if she wa'n't past it—I don't know but she was—and set her down hard in a chair and told her not to come back into the other room, and she minded. She had her hysterics in there till she got tired. When she found out that nobody was comin' to coddle her and do for her she stopped. At least I suppose she did. I had all I could do with poor Aunt Abby tryin' to keep the breath of life in her. The doctor had told me that she was dreadful low, and give me some very strong medicine to give to her in drops real often, and told me real particular about the nourishment. Well, I did as he told me real faithful till she wa'n't able to swaller any longer. Then I had her daughter sent for. I had begun to realize that she wouldn't last any time at all. I hadn't realized it before, though I spoke to Luella the way I did. The doctor he came, and Mrs. Sam Abbot, but when she got there it was too late; her mother was dead. Aunt Abby's daughter just give one look at her mother layin' there, then she turned sort of sharp and sudden and looked at me.

"'Where is she?' says she, and I knew she meant Luella.

"'She's out in the kitchen,' says I. 'She's too nervous to see folks die. She's afraid it will make her sick.'

"The Doctor he speaks up then. He was a young man. Old Doctor Park had died the year before, and this was a young fellow just out of college. 'Mrs. Miller is not strong,' says he, kind of severe, 'and she is quite right in not agitating herself.'

"'You are another, young man; she's got her pretty claw on you,' thinks I, but I didn't say anythin' to him. I just said over to Mrs. Sam Abbot that Luella was in the kitchen, and Mrs. Sam Abbot she went out there, and I went, too, and I never heard anythin' like the way she talked to Luella Miller. I felt pretty hard to Luella myself, but this was more than I ever would have dared to say. Luella she was too scared to go into hysterics. She jest flopped. She seemed to jest shrink away to nothin' in that kitchen chair, with Mrs. Sam Abbot standin' over her and talkin' and tellin' her the truth. I guess the truth was most too much for her and no mistake, because Luella presently actually did faint away, and there wa'n't any sham about it, the way I always suspected there was about them hysterics. She fainted dead away and we had to lay her flat on the floor, and the Doctor he came runnin' out and he said somethin' about a weak heart dreadful fierce to Mrs. Sam Abbot, but she wa'n't a mite scared. She faced him jest as white as even Luella was layin' there lookin' like death and the Doctor feelin' of her pulse.

"'Weak heart,' says she, 'weak heart; weak fiddlesticks! There ain't nothin' weak about that woman. She's got strength enough to hang onto other folks till she kills 'em. Weak? It was my poor mother that was weak: this woman killed her as sure as if she had taken a knife to her.'

"But the Doctor he didn't pay much attention. He was bendin' over Luella layin' there with her yellow hair all streamin' and her pretty pink-and-white face all pale, and her blue eyes like stars gone out, and he was holdin' onto her hand and smoothin' her forehead, and tellin' me to get the brandy in Aunt Abby's room, and I was sure as I wanted to be that Luella had got somebody else to hang onto, now Aunt Abby was gone, and I thought of poor Erastus Miller, and I sort of pitied the poor young Doctor, led away by a pretty face, and I made up my mind I'd see what I could do.

"I waited till Aunt Abby had been dead and buried about a month, and the Doctor was goin' to see Luella steady and folks were beginnin' to talk; then one evenin', when I knew the Doctor had been called out of town and wouldn't be round, I went over to Luella's. I found her all dressed up in a blue muslin with white polka dots on it, and her hair curled jest as pretty, and there wa'n't a young girl in the place could compare with her. There was somethin' about Luella Miller seemed to draw the heart right out of you, but she didn't draw it out of ME. She was settin' rocking in the chair by her sittin'-room window, and Maria Brown had gone home. Maria Brown had been in to help her, or rather to do the work, for Luella wa'n't helped when she didn't do anythin'. Maria Brown was real capable and she didn't have any ties; she wa'n't married, and lived alone, so she'd offered. I couldn't see why she should do the work any more than Luella; she wa'n't any too strong; but she seemed to think she could and Luella seemed to think so, too, so she went over and did all the work—washed, and ironed, and baked, while Luella sat and rocked. Maria didn't live long afterward. She began to fade away just the same fashion the others had. Well, she was warned, but she acted real mad when folks said anythin': said Luella was a poor, abused woman, too delicate to help herself, and they'd ought to be ashamed, and if she died helpin' them that couldn't help themselves she would—and she did.

"'I s'pose Maria has gone home,' says I to Luella, when I had gone in and sat down opposite her.

"'Yes, Maria went half an hour ago, after she had got supper and washed the dishes,' says Luella, in her pretty way.

"'I suppose she has got a lot of work to do in her own house tonight,' says I, kind of bitter, but that was all thrown away on Luella Miller. It seemed to her right that other folks that wa'n't any better able than she was herself should wait on her, and she couldn't get it through her head that anybody should think it WA'N'T right.

"'Yes,' says Luella, real sweet and pretty, 'yes, she said she had to do her washin' tonight. She has let it go for a fortnight along of comin' over here.'

"'Why don't she stay home and do her washin' instead of comin' over here and doin' YOUR work, when you are just as well able, and enough sight more so, than she is to do it?' says I.

"Then Luella she looked at me like a baby who has a rattle shook at it. She sort of laughed as innocent as you please. 'Oh, I can't do the work myself, Miss Anderson,' says she. 'I never did. Maria HAS to do it.'

"Then I spoke out: 'Has to do it I' says I. 'Has to do it!' She don't have to do it, either. Maria Brown has her own home and enough to live on. She ain't beholden to you to come over here and slave for you and kill herself.'

"Luella she jest set and stared at me for all the world like a doll-baby that was so abused that it was comin' to life.

"'Yes,' says I, 'she's killin' herself. She's goin' to die just the way Erastus did, and Lily, and your Aunt Abby. You're killin' her jest as you did them. I don't know what there is about you, but you seem to bring a curse,' says I. 'You kill everybody that is fool enough to care anythin' about you and do for you.'

"She stared at me and she was pretty pale.

"'And Maria ain't the only one you're goin' to kill,' says I. 'You're goin' to kill Doctor Malcom before you're done with him.'

"Then a red colour came flamin' all over her face. 'I ain't goin' to kill him, either,' says she, and she begun to cry.

"'Yes, you BE!' says I. Then I spoke as I had never spoke before. You see, I felt it on account of Erastus. I told her that she hadn't any business to think of another man after she'd been married to one that had died for her: that she was a dreadful woman; and she was, that's true enough, but sometimes I have wondered lately if she knew it—if she wa'n't like a baby with scissors in its hand cuttin' everybody without knowin' what it was doin'.

"Luella she kept gettin' paler and paler, and she never took her eyes off my face. There was somethin' awful about the way she looked at me and never spoke one word. After awhile I quit talkin' and I went home. I watched that night, but her lamp went out before nine o'clock, and when Doctor Malcom came drivin' past and sort of slowed up he see there wa'n't any light and he drove along. I saw her sort of shy out of meetin' the next Sunday, too, so he shouldn't go home with her, and I begun to think mebbe she did have some conscience after all. It was only a week after that that Maria Brown died—sort of sudden at the last, though everybody had seen it was comin'. Well, then there was a good deal of feelin' and pretty dark whispers. Folks said the days of witchcraft had come again, and they were pretty shy of Luella. She acted sort of offish to the Doctor and he didn't go there, and there wa'n't anybody to do anythin' for her. I don't know how she DID get along. I wouldn't go in there and offer to help her—not because I was afraid of dyin' like the rest, but I thought she was just as well able to do her own work as I was to do it for her, and I thought it was about time that she did it and stopped killin' other folks. But it wa'n't very long before folks began to say that Luella herself was goin' into a decline jest the way her husband, and Lily, and Aunt Abby and the others had, and I saw myself that she looked pretty bad. I used to see her goin' past from the store with a bundle as if she could hardly crawl, but I remembered how Erastus used to wait and 'tend when he couldn't hardly put one foot before the other, and I didn't go out to help her.

"But at last one afternoon I saw the Doctor come drivin' up like mad with his medicine chest, and Mrs. Babbit came in after supper and said that Luella was real sick.

"'I'd offer to go in and nurse her,' says she, 'but I've got my children to consider, and mebbe it ain't true what they say, but it's queer how many folks that have done for her have died.'

"I didn't say anythin', but I considered how she had been Erastus's wife and how he had set his eyes by her, and I made up my mind to go in the next mornin', unless she was better, and see what I could do; but the next mornin' I see her at the window, and pretty soon she came steppin' out as spry as you please, and a little while afterward Mrs. Babbit came in and told me that the Doctor had got a girl from out of town, a Sarah Jones, to come there, and she said she was pretty sure that the Doctor was goin' to marry Luella.

"I saw him kiss her in the door that night myself, and I knew it was true. The woman came that afternoon, and the way she flew around was a caution. I don't believe Luella had swept since Maria died. She swept and dusted, and washed and ironed; wet clothes and dusters and carpets were flyin' over there all day, and every time

Luella set her foot out when the Doctor wa'n't there there was that Sarah Jones helpin' of her up and down the steps, as if she hadn't learned to walk.

"Well, everybody knew that Luella and the Doctor were goin' to be married, but it wa'n't long before they began to talk about his lookin' so poorly, jest as they had about the others; and they talked about Sarah Jones, too.

"Well, the Doctor did die, and he wanted to be married first, so as to leave what little he had to Luella, but he died before the minister could get there, and Sarah Jones died a week afterward.

"Well, that wound up everything for Luella Miller. Not another soul in the whole town would lift a finger for her. There got to be a sort of panic. Then she began to droop in good earnest. She used to have to go to the store herself, for Mrs. Babbit was afraid to let Tommy go for her, and I've seen her goin' past and stoppin' every two or three steps to rest. Well, I stood it as long as I could, but one day I see her comin' with her arms full and stoppin' to lean against the Babbit fence, and I run out and took her bundles and carried them to her house. Then I went home and never spoke one word to her though she called after me dreadful kind of pitiful. Well, that night I was taken sick with a chill, and I was sick as I wanted to be for two weeks. Mrs. Babbit had seen me run out to help Luella and she came in and told me I was goin' to die on account of it. I didn't know whether I was or not, but I considered I had done right by Erastus's wife.

"That last two weeks Luella she had a dreadful hard time, I guess. She was pretty sick, and as near as I could make out nobody dared go near her. I don't know as she was really needin' anythin' very much, for there was enough to eat in her house and it was warm weather, and she made out to cook a little flour gruel every day, I know, but I guess she had a hard time, she that had been so petted and done for all her life.

"When I got so I could go out, I went over there one morning. Mrs. Babbit had just come in to say she hadn't seen any smoke and she didn't know but it was somebody's duty to go in, but she couldn't help thinkin' of her children, and I got right up, though I hadn't been out of the house for two weeks, and I went in there, and Luella she was layin' on the bed, and she was dyin'.

"She lasted all that day and into the night. But I sat there after the new doctor had gone away. Nobody else dared to go there. It was about midnight that I left her for a minute to run home and get some medicine I had been takin', for I begun to feel rather bad.

"It was a full moon that night, and just as I started out of my door to cross the street back to Luella's, I stopped short, for I saw something."

Lydia Anderson at this juncture always said with a certain defiance that she did not expect to be believed, and then proceeded in a hushed voice:

"I saw what I saw, and I know I saw it, and I will swear on my death bed that I saw it. I saw Luella Miller and Erastus Miller, and Lily, and Aunt Abby, and Maria, and the Doctor, and Sarah, all goin' out of her door, and all but Luella shone white in the moonlight, and they were all helpin' her along till she seemed to fairly fly in the midst of them. Then it all disappeared. I stood a minute with my heart poundin', then I went over there. I thought of goin' for Mrs. Babbit, but I thought she'd be afraid. So I went alone, though I knew what had happened. Luella was layin' real peaceful, dead on her bed."

This was the story that the old woman, Lydia Anderson, told, but the sequel was told by the people who survived her, and this is the tale which has become folklore in the village.

Lydia Anderson died when she was eighty-seven. She had continued wonderfully hale and hearty for one of her years until about two weeks before her death.

One bright moonlight evening she was sitting beside a window in her parlour when she made a sudden exclamation, and was out of the house and across the street before the neighbour who was taking care of her could stop her. She followed as fast as possible and found Lydia Anderson stretched on the ground before the door of Luella Miller's deserted house, and she was quite dead.

The next night there was a red gleam of fire athwart the moonlight and the old house of Luella Miller was burned to the ground. Nothing is now left of it except a few old cellar stones and a lilac bush, and in summer a helpless trail of morning glories among the weeds, which might be considered emblematic of Luella herself.

THE SOUTHWEST CHAMBER

"That school-teacher from Acton is coming today," said the elder Miss Gill, Sophia.

"So she is," assented the younger Miss Gill, Amanda.

"I have decided to put her in the southwest chamber," said Sophia.

Amanda looked at her sister with an expression of mingled doubt and terror. "You don't suppose she would—" she began hesitatingly.

"Would what?" demanded Sophia, sharply. She was more incisive than her sister. Both were below the medium height, and stout, but Sophia was firm where Amanda was flabby. Amanda wore a baggy old muslin (it was a hot day), and Sophia was uncompromisingly hooked up in a starched and boned cambric over her high shelving figure.

"I didn't know but she would object to sleeping in that room, as long as Aunt Harriet died there such a little time ago," faltered Amanda.

"Well!" said Sophia, "of all the silly notions! If you are going to pick out rooms in this house where nobody has died, for the boarders, you'll have your hands full. Grandfather Ackley had seven children; four of them died here to my certain knowledge, besides grandfather and grandmother. I think Great-grandmother Ackley, grandfather's mother, died here, too; she must have; and Great-grandfather Ackley, and grandfather's unmarried sister, Great-aunt Fanny Ackley. I don't believe there's a room nor a bed in this house that somebody hasn't passed away in."

"Well, I suppose I am silly to think of it, and she had better go in there," said Amanda.

"I know she had. The northeast room is small and hot, and she's stout and likely to feel the heat, and she's saved money and is able to board out summers, and maybe she'll come here another year if she's well accommodated," said Sophia. "Now I guess you'd better go in there and see if any dust has settled on anything since it was cleaned, and open the west windows and let the sun in, while I see to that cake."

Amanda went to her task in the southwest chamber while her sister stepped heavily down the back stairs on her way to the kitchen.

"It seems to me you had better open the bed while you air and dust, then make it up again," she called back.

"Yes, sister," Amanda answered, shudderingly.

Nobody knew how this elderly woman with the untrammeled imagination of a child dreaded to enter the southwest chamber, and yet she could not have told why she had the dread. She had entered and occupied rooms which had been once tenanted by persons now dead. The room which had been hers in the little house in which she and her sister had lived before coming here had been her dead mother's. She had never reflected upon the fact with anything but loving awe and reverence. There had never been any fear. But this was different. She entered and her heart beat thickly in her ears. Her hands were cold. The room was a very large one. The four windows, two facing south, two west, were closed, the blinds also. The room was in a film of green gloom. The furniture loomed out vaguely. The gilt frame of a blurred old engraving on the wall caught a little light. The white counterpane on the bed showed like a blank page.

Amanda crossed the room, opened with a straining motion of her thin back and shoulders one of the west windows, and threw back the blind. Then the room revealed itself an apartment full of an aged and worn but no less valid state. Pieces of old mahogany swelled forth; a peacock-patterned chintz draped the bedstead. This chintz also covered a great easy chair which had been the favourite seat of the former occupant of the room. The closet door stood ajar. Amanda noticed that with wonder. There was a glimpse of purple drapery floating from a peg inside the closet. Amanda went across and took down the garment hanging there. She wondered how her sister had happened to leave it when she cleaned the room. It was an old loose gown which had belonged to her aunt. She took it down, shuddering, and closed the closet door after a fearful glance into its dark depths. It was a long closet with a strong odour of lovage. The Aunt Harriet had had a habit of eating lovage and had carried it constantly in her pocket. There was very likely some of the pleasant root in the pocket of the musty purple gown which Amanda threw over the easy chair.

Amanda perceived the odour with a start as if before an actual presence. Odour seems in a sense a vital part of a personality. It can survive the flesh to which it has clung like a persistent shadow, seeming to have in itself something of the substance of that to which it pertained. Amanda was always conscious of this fragrance of lovage as she tidied the room. She dusted the heavy mahogany pieces punctiliously after she had opened the bed as her sister had directed. She spread fresh towels over the wash-stand and the bureau; she made the bed. Then she thought to take the purple gown from the easy chair and carry it to the garret and put it in the trunk with the other articles of the dead woman's wardrobe which had been packed away there; BUT THE PURPLE GOWN WAS NOT ON THE CHAIR!

Amanda Gill was not a woman of strong convictions even as to her own actions. She directly thought that possibly she had been mistaken and had not removed it from the closet. She glanced at the closet door and saw with surprise that it was open, and she had thought she had closed it, but she instantly was not sure of that. So she entered the closet and looked for the purple gown. IT WAS NOT THERE!

Amanda Gill went feebly out of the closet and looked at the easy chair again. The purple gown was not there! She looked wildly around the room. She went down on her trembling knees and peered under the bed, she opened the bureau drawers, she looked again in the closet. Then she stood in the middle of the floor and fairly wrung her hands.

"What does it mean?" she said in a shocked whisper.

She had certainly seen that loose purple gown of her dead Aunt Harriet's.

There is a limit at which self-refutation must stop in any sane person. Amanda Gill had reached it. She knew that she had seen that purple gown in that closet; she knew that she had removed it and put it on the easy chair. She also knew that she had not taken it out of the room. She felt a curious sense of being inverted mentally. It was as if all her traditions and laws of life were on their heads. Never in her simple record had any garment not remained where she had placed it unless removed by some palpable human agency.

Then the thought occurred to her that possibly her sister Sophia might have entered the room unobserved while her back was turned and removed the dress. A sensation of relief came over her. Her blood seemed to flow back into its usual channels; the tension of her nerves relaxed.

"How silly I am," she said aloud.

She hurried out and downstairs into the kitchen where Sophia was making cake, stirring with splendid circular sweeps of a wooden spoon a creamy yellow mass. She looked up as her sister entered.

"Have you got it done?" said she.

"Yes," replied Amanda. Then she hesitated. A sudden terror overcame her. It did not seem as if it were at all probable that Sophia had left that foamy cake mixture a second to go to Aunt Harriet's chamber and remove that purple gown.

"Well," said Sophia, "if you have got that done I wish you would take hold and string those beans. The first thing we know there won't be time to boil them for dinner."

Amanda moved toward the pan of beans on the table, then she looked at her sister.

"Did you come up in Aunt Harriet's room while I was there?" she asked weakly.

She knew while she asked what the answer would be.

"Up in Aunt Harriet's room? Of course I didn't. I couldn't leave this cake without having it fall. You know that well enough. Why?"

"Nothing," replied Amanda.

Suddenly she realized that she could not tell her sister what had happened, for before the utter absurdity of the whole thing her belief in her own reason quailed. She knew what Sophia would say if she told her. She could hear her.

"Amanda Gill, have you gone stark staring mad?"

She resolved that she would never tell Sophia. She dropped into a chair and begun shelling the beans with nerveless fingers. Sophia looked at her curiously.

"Amanda Gill, what on earth ails you?" she asked.

"Nothing," replied Amanda. She bent her head very low over the green pods.

"Yes, there is, too! You are as white as a sheet, and your hands are shaking so you can hardly string those beans. I did think you had more sense, Amanda Gill."

"I don't know what you mean, Sophia."

"Yes, you do know what I mean, too; you needn't pretend you don't. Why did you ask me if I had been in that room, and why do you act so queer?"

Amanda hesitated. She had been trained to truth. Then she lied.

"I wondered if you'd noticed how it had leaked in on the paper over by the bureau, that last rain," said she.

"What makes you look so pale then?"

"I don't know. I guess the heat sort of overcame me."

"I shouldn't think it could have been very hot in that room when it had been shut up so long," said Sophia.

She was evidently not satisfied, but then the grocer came to the door and the matter dropped.

For the next hour the two women were very busy. They kept no servant. When they had come into possession of this fine old place by the death of their aunt it had seemed a doubtful blessing. There was not a cent with which to pay for repairs and taxes and insurance, except the twelve hundred dollars which they had obtained from the sale of the little house in which they had been born and lived all their lives. There had been a division in the old Ackley family years before. One of the daughters had married against her mother's wish and had been disinherited. She had married a poor man by the name of Gill, and shared his humble lot in sight of her former home and her sister and mother living in prosperity, until she had borne three daughters; then she died, worn out with overwork and worry.

The mother and the elder sister had been pitiless to the last. Neither had ever spoken to her since she left her home the night of her marriage. They were hard women.

The three daughters of the disinherited sister had lived quiet and poor, but not actually needy lives. Jane, the middle daughter, had married, and died in less than a year. Amanda and Sophia had taken the girl baby she left when the father married again. Sophia had taught a primary school for many years; she had saved enough to buy the little house in which they lived. Amanda had crocheted lace, and embroidered flannel, and made tidies and pincushions, and had earned enough for her clothes and the child's, little Flora Scott.

Their father, William Gill, had died before they were thirty, and now in their late middle life had come the death of the aunt to whom they had never spoken, although they had often seen her, who had lived in solitary state in the old Ackley mansion until she was more than eighty. There had been no will, and they were the only heirs with the exception of young Flora Scott, the daughter of the dead sister.

Sophia and Amanda thought directly of Flora when they knew of the inheritance.

"It will be a splendid thing for her; she will have enough to live on when we are gone," Sophia said.

She had promptly decided what was to be done. The small house was to be sold, and they were to move into the old Ackley house and take boarders to pay for its keeping. She scouted the idea of selling it. She had an enormous family pride. She had always held her head high when she had walked past that fine old mansion, the cradle of her race, which she was forbidden to enter. She was unmoved when the lawyer who was advising her disclosed to her the fact that Harriet Ackley had used every cent of the Ackley money.

"I realize that we have to work," said she, "but my sister and I have determined to keep the place."

That was the end of the discussion. Sophia and Amanda Gill had been living in the old Ackley house a fortnight, and they had three boarders: an elderly widow with a comfortable income, a young congregationalist clergyman, and the middle-aged single woman who had charge of the village library. Now the school-teacher from Acton, Miss Louisa Stark, was expected for the summer, and would make four.

Sophia considered that they were comfortably provided for. Her wants and her sister's were very few, and even the niece, although a young girl, had small expenses, since her wardrobe was supplied for years to come from that of the deceased aunt. There were stored away in the garret of the Ackley house enough voluminous black silks and satins and bombazines to keep her clad in somber richness for years to come.

Flora was a very gentle girl, with large, serious blue eyes, a seldom-smiling, pretty mouth, and smooth flaxen hair. She was delicate and very young—sixteen on her next birthday.

She came home soon now with her parcels of sugar and tea from the grocer's. She entered the kitchen gravely and deposited them on the table by which her Aunt Amanda was seated stringing beans. Flora wore an obsolete turban-shaped hat of black straw which had belonged to the dead aunt; it set high like a crown, revealing her forehead. Her dress was an ancient purple-and-white print, too long and too large except over the chest, where it held her like a straight waistcoat.

"You had better take off your hat, Flora," said Sophia. She turned suddenly to Amanda. "Did you fill the water-pitcher in that chamber for the schoolteacher?" she asked severely. She was quite sure that Amanda had not filled the water-pitcher.

Amanda blushed and started guiltily. "I declare, I don't believe I did," said she.

"I didn't think you had," said her sister with sarcastic emphasis.

"Flora, you go up to the room that was your Great-aunt Harriet's, and take the water-pitcher off the wash-stand and fill it with water. Be real careful, and don't break the pitcher, and don't spill the water."

"In THAT chamber?" asked Flora. She spoke very quietly, but her face changed a little.

"Yes, in that chamber," returned her Aunt Sophia sharply. "Go right along."

Flora went, and her light footstep was heard on the stairs. Very soon she returned with the blue-and-white water-pitcher and filled it carefully at the kitchen sink.

"Now be careful and not spill it," said Sophia as she went out of the room carrying it gingerly.

Amanda gave a timidly curious glance at her; she wondered if she had seen the purple gown.

Then she started, for the village stagecoach was seen driving around to the front of the house. The house stood on a corner.

"Here, Amanda, you look better than I do; you go and meet her," said Sophia. "I'll just put the cake in the pan and get it in the oven and I'll come. Show her right up to her room."

Amanda removed her apron hastily and obeyed. Sophia hurried with her cake, pouring it into the baking-tins. She had just put it in the oven, when the door opened and Flora entered carrying the blue water-pitcher.

"What are you bringing down that pitcher again for?" asked Sophia.

"She wants some water, and Aunt Amanda sent me," replied Flora.

Her pretty pale face had a bewildered expression.

"For the land sake, she hasn't used all that great pitcherful of water so quick?"

"There wasn't any water in it," replied Flora.

Her high, childish forehead was contracted slightly with a puzzled frown as she looked at her aunt.

"Wasn't any water in it?"

"No, ma'am."

"Didn't I see you filling the pitcher with water not ten minutes ago, I want to know?"

"Yes, ma'am."

"What did you do with that water?"

"Nothing."

"Did you carry that pitcherful of water up to that room and set it on the washstand?"

"Yes, ma'am."

"Didn't you spill it?"

"No, ma'am."

"Now, Flora Scott, I want the truth! Did you fill that pitcher with water and carry it up there, and wasn't there any there when she came to use it?"

"Yes, ma'am."

"Let me see that pitcher." Sophia examined the pitcher. It was not only perfectly dry from top to bottom, but even a little dusty. She turned severely on the young girl. "That shows," said she, "you did not fill the pitcher at all. You let the water run at the side because you didn't want to carry it upstairs. I am ashamed of you. It's bad enough to be so lazy, but when it comes to not telling the truth—"

The young girl's face broke up suddenly into piteous confusion, and her blue eyes became filmy with tears.

"I did fill the pitcher, honest," she faltered, "I did, Aunt Sophia. You ask Aunt Amanda."

"I'll ask nobody. This pitcher is proof enough. Water don't go off and leave the pitcher dusty on the inside if it was put in ten minutes ago. Now you fill that pitcher full quick, and you carry it upstairs, and if you spill a drop there'll be something besides talk."

Flora filled the pitcher, with the tears falling over her cheeks. She sniveled softly as she went out, balancing it carefully against her slender hip. Sophia followed her.

"Stop crying," said she sharply; "you ought to be ashamed of yourself. What do you suppose Miss Louisa Stark will think. No water in her pitcher in the first place, and then you come back crying as if you didn't want to get it."

In spite of herself, Sophia's voice was soothing. She was very fond of the girl. She followed her up the stairs to the chamber where Miss Louisa Stark was waiting for the water to remove the soil of travel. She had removed her bonnet, and its tuft of red geraniums lightened the obscurity of the mahogany dresser. She had placed her little beaded cape carefully on the bed. She was replying to a tremulous remark of Amanda's, who was nearly fainting from the new mystery of the water-pitcher, that it was warm and she suffered a good deal in warm weather.

Louisa Stark was stout and solidly built. She was much larger than either of the Gill sisters. She was a masterly woman inured to command from years of school-teaching. She carried her swelling bulk with majesty; even her face, moist and red with the heat, lost nothing of its dignity of expression.

She was standing in the middle of the floor with an air which gave the effect of her standing upon an elevation. She turned when Sophia and Flora, carrying the water-pitcher, entered.

"This is my sister Sophia," said Amanda tremulously.

Sophia advanced, shook hands with Miss Louisa Stark and bade her welcome and hoped she would like her room. Then she moved toward the closet. "There is a nice large closet in this room—the best closet in the house. You might have your trunk—" she said, then she stopped short.

The closet door was ajar, and a purple garment seemed suddenly to swing into view as if impelled by some wind.

"Why, here is something left in this closet," Sophia said in a mortified tone. "I thought all those things had been taken away."

She pulled down the garment with a jerk, and as she did so Amanda passed her in a weak rush for the door.

"I am afraid your sister is not well," said the school-teacher from Acton. "She looked very pale when you took that dress down. I noticed it at once. Hadn't you better go and see what the matter is? She may be going to faint."

"She is not subject to fainting spells," replied Sophia, but she followed Amanda.

She found her in the room which they occupied together, lying on the bed, very pale and gasping. She leaned over her.

"Amanda, what is the matter; don't you feel well?" she asked.

"I feel a little faint."

Sophia got a camphor bottle and began rubbing her sister's forehead.

"Do you feel better?" she said.

Amanda nodded.

"I guess it was that green apple pie you ate this noon," said Sophia. "I declare, what did I do with that dress of Aunt Harriet's? I guess if you feel better I'll just run and get it and take it up garret. I'll stop in here again when I come down. You'd better lay still. Flora can bring you up a cup of tea. I wouldn't try to eat any supper."

Sophia's tone as she left the room was full of loving concern. Presently she returned; she looked disturbed, but angrily so. There was not the slightest hint of any fear in her expression.

"I want to know," said she, looking sharply and quickly around, "if I brought that purple dress in here, after all?"

"I didn't see you," replied Amanda.

"I must have. It isn't in that chamber, nor the closet. You aren't lying on it, are you?"

"I lay down before you came in," replied Amanda.

"So you did. Well, I'll go and look again."

Presently Amanda heard her sister's heavy step on the garret stairs. Then she returned with a queer defiant expression on her face.

"I carried it up garret, after all, and put it in the trunk," said, she. "I declare, I forgot it. I suppose your being faint sort of put it out of my head. There it was, folded up just as nice, right where I put it."

Sophia's mouth was set; her eyes upon her sister's scared, agitated face were full of hard challenge.

"Yes," murmured Amanda.

"I must go right down and see to that cake," said Sophia, going out of the room. "If you don't feel well, you pound on the floor with the umbrella."

Amanda looked after her. She knew that Sophia had not put that purple dress of her dead Aunt Harriet in the trunk in the garret.

Meantime Miss Louisa Stark was settling herself in the southwest chamber. She unpacked her trunk and hung her dresses carefully in the closet. She filled the bureau drawers with nicely folded linen and small articles of dress. She was a very punctilious woman. She put on a black India silk dress with purple flowers. She combed her grayish-blond hair in smooth ridges back from her broad forehead. She pinned her lace at her throat with a brooch, very handsome, although somewhat obsolete—a bunch of pearl grapes on black onyx, set in gold filagree. She had purchased it several years ago with a considerable portion of the stipend from her spring term of school-teaching.

As she surveyed herself in the little swing mirror surmounting the old-fashioned mahogany bureau she suddenly bent forward and looked closely at the brooch. It seemed to her that something was wrong with it. As she looked she became sure. Instead of the familiar bunch of pearl grapes on the black onyx, she saw a knot of blonde and black hair under glass surrounded by a border of twisted gold. She felt a thrill of horror, though she could not tell why. She unpinned the brooch, and it was her own familiar one, the pearl grapes and the onyx. "How very foolish I am," she thought. She thrust the pin in the laces at her throat and again looked at herself in the glass, and there it was again—the knot of blond and black hair and the twisted gold.

Louisa Stark looked at her own large, firm face above the brooch and it was full of terror and dismay which were new to it. She straightway began to wonder if there could be anything wrong with her mind. She remembered that an aunt of her mother's had been insane. A sort of fury with herself possessed her. She stared at the brooch in the glass with eyes at once angry and terrified. Then she removed it again and there was her own old brooch. Finally she thrust the gold pin through the lace again, fastened it and turning a defiant back on the glass, went down to supper.

At the supper table she met the other boarders—the elderly widow, the young clergyman and the middle-aged librarian. She viewed the elderly widow with reserve, the clergyman with respect, the middle-aged librarian with suspicion. The latter wore a very youthful shirt-waist, and her hair in a girlish fashion which the school-teacher, who twisted hers severely from the straining roots at the nape of her neck to the small, smooth coil at the top, condemned as straining after effects no longer hers by right.

The librarian, who had a quick acridness of manner, addressed her, asking what room she had, and asked the second time in spite of the school-teacher's evident reluctance to hear her. She even, since she sat next to her, nudged her familiarly in her rigid black silk side.

"What room are you in, Miss Stark?" said she.

"I am at a loss how to designate the room," replied Miss Stark stiffly.

"Is it the big southwest room?"

"It evidently faces in that direction," said Miss Stark.

The librarian, whose name was Eliza Lippincott, turned abruptly to Miss Amanda Gill, over whose delicate face a curious colour compounded of flush and pallour was stealing.

"What room did your aunt die in, Miss Amanda?" asked she abruptly.

Amanda cast a terrified glance at her sister, who was serving a second plate of pudding for the minister.

"That room," she replied feebly.

"That's what I thought," said the librarian with a certain triumph. "I calculated that must be the room she died in, for it's the best room in the house, and you haven't put anybody in it before. Somehow the room that anybody has died in lately is generally the last room that anybody is put in. I suppose YOU are so strong-minded you don't object to sleeping in a room where anybody died a few weeks ago?" she inquired of Louisa Stark with sharp eyes on her face.

"No, I do not," replied Miss stark with emphasis.

"Nor in the same bed?" persisted Eliza Lippincott with a kittenish reflection.

The young minister looked up from his pudding. He was very spiritual, but he had had poor pickings in his previous boarding place, and he could not help a certain abstract enjoyment over Miss Gill's cooking.

"You would certainly not be afraid, Miss Lippincott?" he remarked, with his gentle, almost caressing inflection of tone. "You do not for a minute believe that a higher power would allow any manifestation on the part of a disembodied spirit—who we trust is in her heavenly home—to harm one of His servants?"

"Oh, Mr. Dunn, of course not," replied Eliza Lippincott with a blush. "Of course not. I never meant to imply—"

"I could not believe you did," said the minister gently. He was very young, but he already had a wrinkle of permanent anxiety between his eyes and a smile of permanent ingratiation on his lips. The lines of the smile were as deeply marked as the wrinkle.

"Of course dear Miss Harriet Gill was a professing Christian," remarked the widow, "and I don't suppose a professing Christian would come back and scare folks if she could. I wouldn't be a mite afraid to sleep in that room; I'd rather have it than the one I've got. If I was afraid to sleep in a room where a good woman died, I wouldn't tell of it. If I saw things or heard things I'd think the fault must be with my own guilty conscience." Then she turned to Miss Stark. "Any time you feel timid in that room I'm ready and willing to change with you," said she.

"Thank you; I have no desire to change. I am perfectly satisfied with my room," replied Miss Stark with freezing dignity, which was thrown away upon the widow.

"Well," said she, "any time, if you should feel timid, you know what to do. I've got a real nice room; it faces east and gets the morning sun, but it isn't so nice as yours, according to my way of thinking. I'd rather take my chances any day in a room anybody had died in than in one that was hot in summer. I'm more afraid of a sunstroke than of spooks, for my part."

Miss Sophia Gill, who had not spoken one word, but whose mouth had become more and more rigidly compressed, suddenly rose from the table, forcing the minister to leave a little pudding, at which he glanced regretfully.

Miss Louisa Stark did not sit down in the parlour with the other boarders. She went straight to her room. She felt tired after her journey, and meditated a loose wrapper and writing a few letters quietly before she went to bed. Then, too, she was conscious of a feeling that if she delayed, the going there at all might assume more terrifying proportions. She was full of defiance against herself and her own lurking weakness.

So she went resolutely and entered the southwest chamber. There was through the room a soft twilight. She could dimly discern everything, the white satin scroll-work on the wall paper and the white counterpane on the bed being most evident. Consequently both arrested her attention first. She saw against the wall-paper directly facing the door the waist of her best black satin dress hung over a picture.

"That is very strange," she said to herself, and again a thrill of vague horror came over her.

She knew, or thought she knew, that she had put that black satin dress waist away nicely folded between towels in her trunk. She was very choice of her black satin dress.

She took down the black waist and laid it on the bed preparatory to folding it, but when she attempted to do so she discovered that the two sleeves were firmly sewed together. Louisa Stark stared at the sewed sleeves. "What does this mean?" she asked herself. She examined the sewing carefully; the stitches were small, and even, and firm, of black silk.

She looked around the room. On the stand beside the bed was something which she had not noticed before: a little old-fashioned work-box with a picture of a little boy in a pinafore on the top. Beside this work-box lay, as if just laid down by the user, a spool of black silk, a pair of scissors, and a large steel thimble with a hole in the top, after an old style. Louisa stared at these, then at the sleeves of her dress. She moved toward the door. For a moment she thought that this was something legitimate about which she might demand information; then she became doubtful. Suppose that work-box had been there all the time; suppose she had forgotten; suppose she herself had done this absurd thing, or suppose that she had not, what was to hinder the others from thinking so; what was to hinder a doubt being cast upon her own memory and reasoning powers?

Louisa Stark had been on the verge of a nervous breakdown in spite of her iron constitution and her great will power. No woman can teach school for forty years with absolute impunity. She was more credulous as to her own possible failings than she had ever been in her whole life. She was cold with horror and terror, and yet not so much horror and terror of the supernatural as of her own self. The weakness of belief in the supernatural was nearly impossible for this strong nature. She could more easily believe in her own failing powers.

"I don't know but I'm going to be like Aunt Marcia," she said to herself, and her fat face took on a long rigidity of fear.

She started toward the mirror to unfasten her dress, then she remembered the strange circumstance of the brooch and stopped short. Then she straightened herself defiantly and marched up to the bureau and looked in the glass. She saw reflected therein, fastening the lace at her throat, the old-fashioned thing of a large oval, a knot of fair and black hair under glass, set in a rim of twisted gold. She unfastened it with trembling fingers and looked at it. It was her own brooch, the cluster of pearl grapes on black onyx. Louisa Stark placed the trinket in its little box on the nest of pink cotton and put it away in the bureau drawer. Only death could disturb her habit of order.

Her fingers were so cold they felt fairly numb as she unfastened her dress; she staggered when she slipped it over her head. She went to the closet to hang it up and recoiled. A strong smell of lovage came in her nostrils; a purple gown near the door swung softly against her face as if impelled by some wind from within. All the pegs were filled with garments not her own, mostly of somber black, but there were some strange-patterned silk things and satins.

Suddenly Louisa Stark recovered her nerve. This, she told herself, was something distinctly tangible. Somebody had been taking liberties with her wardrobe. Somebody had been hanging some one else's clothes in her closet. She hastily slipped on her dress again and marched straight down to the parlour. The people were seated there; the widow and the minister were playing backgammon. The librarian was watching them. Miss Amanda Gill was mending beside the large lamp on the centre table. They all looked up with amazement as Louisa Stark entered. There was something strange in her expression. She noticed none of them except Amanda.

"Where is your sister?" she asked peremptorily of her.

"She's in the kitchen mixing up bread," Amanda quavered; "is there anything—" But the school-teacher was gone.

She found Sophia Gill standing by the kitchen table kneading dough with dignity. The young girl Flora was bringing some flour from the pantry. She stopped and stared at Miss Stark, and her pretty, delicate young face took on an expression of alarm.

Miss Stark opened at once upon the subject in her mind.

"Miss Gill," said she, with her utmost school-teacher manner, "I wish to inquire why you have had my own clothes removed from the closet in my room and others substituted?"

Sophia Gill stood with her hands fast in the dough, regarding her. Her own face paled slowly and reluctantly, her mouth stiffened.

"What? I don't quite understand what you mean, Miss Stark," said she.

"My clothes are not in the closet in my room and it is full of things which do not belong to me," said Louisa Stark.

"Bring me that flour," said Sophia sharply to the young girl, who obeyed, casting timid, startled glances at Miss Stark as she passed her. Sophia Gill began rubbing her hands clear of the dough. "I am sure I know nothing about it," she said with a certain tempered asperity. "Do you know anything about it, Flora?"

"Oh, no, I don't know anything about it, Aunt Sophia," answered the young girl, fluttering.

Then Sophia turned to Miss Stark. "I'll go upstairs with you, Miss Stark," said she, "and see what the trouble is. There must be some mistake." She spoke stiffly with constrained civility.

"Very well," said Miss Stark with dignity. Then she and Miss Sophia went upstairs. Flora stood staring after them.

Sophia and Louisa Stark went up to the southwest chamber. The closet door was shut. Sophia threw it open, then she looked at

Miss Stark. On the pegs hung the schoolteacher's own garments in ordinary array.

"I can't see that there is anything wrong," remarked Sophia grimly.

Miss Stark strove to speak but she could not. She sank down on the nearest chair. She did not even attempt to defend herself. She saw her own clothes in the closet. She knew there had been no time for any human being to remove those which she thought she had seen and put hers in their places. She knew it was impossible. Again the awful horror of herself overwhelmed her.

"You must have been mistaken," she heard Sophia say.

She muttered something, she scarcely knew what. Sophia then went out of the room. Presently she undressed and went to bed. In the morning she did not go down to breakfast, and when Sophia came to inquire, requested that the stage be ordered for the noon train. She said that she was sorry, but was ill, and feared lest she might be worse, and she felt that she must return home at once. She looked ill, and could not take even the toast and tea which Sophia had prepared for her. Sophia felt a certain pity for her, but it was largely mixed with indignation. She felt that she knew the true reason for the school-teacher's illness and sudden departure, and it incensed her.

"If folks are going to act like fools we shall never be able to keep this house," she said to Amanda after Miss Stark had gone; and Amanda knew what she meant.

Directly the widow, Mrs. Elvira Simmons, knew that the school-teacher had gone and the southwest room was vacant, she begged to have it in exchange for her own. Sophia hesitated a moment; she eyed the widow sharply. There was something about the large, roseate face worn in firm lines of humour and decision which reassured her.

"I have no objection, Mrs. Simmons," said she, "if—"

"If what?" asked the widow.

"If you have common sense enough not to keep fussing because the room happens to be the one my aunt died in," said Sophia bluntly.

"Fiddlesticks!" said the widow, Mrs. Elvira Simmons.

That very afternoon she moved into the southwest chamber. The young girl Flora assisted her, though much against her will.

"Now I want you to carry Mrs. Simmons' dresses into the closet in that room and hang them up nicely, and see that she has everything she wants," said Sophia Gill. "And you can change the bed and put on fresh sheets. What are you looking at me that way for?"

"Oh, Aunt Sophia, can't I do something else?"

"What do you want to do something else for?"

"I am afraid."

"Afraid of what? I should think you'd hang your head. No; you go right in there and do what I tell you."

Pretty soon Flora came running into the sitting-room where Sophia was, as pale as death, and in her hand she held a queer, old-fashioned frilled nightcap.

"What's that?" demanded Sophia.

"I found it under the pillow."

"What pillow?"

"In the southwest room."

Sophia took it and looked at it sternly.

"It's Great-aunt Harriet's," said Flora faintly.

"You run down street and do that errand at the grocer's for me and I'll see that room," said Sophia with dignity. She carried the nightcap away and put it in the trunk in the garret where she had supposed it stored with the rest of the dead woman's belongings. Then she went into the southwest chamber and made the bed and assisted Mrs. Simmons to move, and there was no further incident.

The widow was openly triumphant over her new room. She talked a deal about it at the dinner-table.

"It is the best room in the house, and I expect you all to be envious of me," said she.

"And you are sure you don't feel afraid of ghosts?" said the librarian.

"Ghosts!" repeated the widow with scorn. "If a ghost comes I'll send her over to you. You are just across the hall from the southwest room."

"You needn't," returned Eliza Lippincott with a shudder. "I wouldn't sleep in that room, after—" she checked herself with an eye on the minister.

"After what?" asked the widow.

"Nothing," replied Eliza Lippincott in an embarrassed fashion.

"I trust Miss Lippincott has too good sense and too great faith to believe in anything of that sort," said the minister.

"I trust so, too," replied Eliza hurriedly.

"You did see or hear something—now what was it, I want to know?" said the widow that evening when they were alone in the parlour. The minister had gone to make a call.

Eliza hesitated.

"What was it?" insisted the widow.

"Well," said Eliza hesitatingly, "if you'll promise not to tell."

"Yes, I promise; what was it?"

"Well, one day last week, just before the school-teacher came, I went in that room to see if there were any clouds. I wanted to wear my gray dress, and I was afraid it was going to rain, so I wanted to look at the sky at all points, so I went in there, and—"

"And what?"

"Well, you know that chintz over the bed, and the valance, and the easy chair; what pattern should you say it was?"

"Why, peacocks on a blue ground. Good land, I shouldn't think any one who had ever seen that would forget it."

"Peacocks on a blue ground, you are sure?"

"Of course I am. Why?"

"Only when I went in there that afternoon it was not peacocks on a blue ground; it was great red roses on a yellow ground."

"Why, what do you mean?"

"What I say."

"Did Miss Sophia have it changed?"

"No. I went in there again an hour later and the peacocks were there."

"You didn't see straight the first time."

"I expected you would say that."

"The peacocks are there now; I saw them just now."

"Yes, I suppose so; I suppose they flew back."

"But they couldn't."

"Looks as if they did."

"Why, how could such a thing be? It couldn't be."

"Well, all I know is those peacocks were gone for an hour that afternoon and the red roses on the yellow ground were there instead."

The widow stared at her a moment, then she began to laugh rather hysterically.

"Well," said she, "I guess I sha'n't give up my nice room for any such tomfoolery as that. I guess I would just as soon have red roses on a yellow ground as peacocks on a blue; but there's no use talking, you couldn't have seen straight. How could such a thing have happened?"

"I don't know," said Eliza Lippincott; "but I know I wouldn't sleep in that room if you'd give me a thousand dollars."

"Well, I would," said the widow, "and I'm going to."

When Mrs. Simmons went to the southwest chamber that night she cast a glance at the bed-hanging and the easy chair. There were the peacocks on the blue ground. She gave a contemptuous thought to Eliza Lippincott.

"I don't believe but she's getting nervous," she thought. "I wonder if any of her family have been out at all."

But just before Mrs. Simmons was ready to get into bed she looked again at the hangings and the easy chair, and there were the red roses on the yellow ground instead of the peacocks on the blue. She looked long and sharply. Then she shut her eyes, and then opened them and looked. She still saw the red roses. Then she crossed the room, turned her back to the bed, and looked out at the night from the south window. It was clear and the full moon was shining. She watched it a moment sailing over the dark blue in its nimbus of gold. Then she looked around at the bed hangings. She still saw the red roses on the yellow ground.

Mrs. Simmons was struck in her most vulnerable point. This apparent contradiction of the reasonable as manifested in such a commonplace thing as chintz of a bed-hanging affected this ordinarily unimaginative woman as no ghostly appearance could have done. Those red roses on the yellow ground were to her much more ghostly than any strange figure clad in the white robes of the grave entering the room.

She took a step toward the door, then she turned with a resolute air. "As for going downstairs and owning up I'm scared and having that Lippincott girl crowing over me, I won't for any red roses instead of peacocks. I guess they can't hurt me, and as long as we've both of us seen 'em I guess we can't both be getting loony," she said.

Mrs. Elvira Simmons blew out her light and got into bed and lay staring out between the chintz hangings at the moonlit room. She said her prayers in bed always as being more comfortable, and presumably just as acceptable in the case of a faithful servant with a stout habit of body. Then after a little she fell asleep; she was of too practical a nature to be kept long awake by anything which had no power of actual bodily effect upon her. No stress of the spirit had ever disturbed her slumbers. So she slumbered between the red roses, or the peacocks, she did not know which.

But she was awakened about midnight by a strange sensation in her throat. She had dreamed that some one with long white fingers was strangling her, and she saw bending over her the face of an old woman in a white cap. When she waked there was no old woman, the room was almost as light as day in the full moonlight, and looked very peaceful; but the strangling sensation at her throat continued, and besides that, her face and ears felt muffled. She put up her hand and felt that her head was covered with a ruffled nightcap tied under her chin so tightly that it was exceedingly uncomfortable. A great qualm of horror shot over her. She tore the thing off frantically and flung it from her with a convulsive effort as if it had been a spider. She gave, as she did so, a quick, short scream of terror. She sprang out of bed and was going toward the door, when she stopped.

It had suddenly occurred to her that Eliza Lippincott might have entered the room and tied on the cap while she was asleep. She had not locked her door. She looked in the closet, under the bed; there was no one there. Then she tried to open the door, but to her astonishment found that it was locked—bolted on the inside. "I must have locked it, after all," she reflected with wonder, for she never locked her door. Then she could scarcely conceal from herself that there was something out of the usual about it all. Certainly no one could have entered the room and departed locking the door on the inside. She could not control the long shiver of horror that crept over her, but she was still resolute. She resolved that she would throw the cap out of the window. "I'll see if I have tricks like that played on me, I don't care who does it," said she quite aloud. She was still unable to believe wholly in the supernatural. The idea of some human agency was still in her mind, filling her with anger.

She went toward the spot where she had thrown the cap—she had stepped over it on her way to the door—but it was not there. She searched the whole room, lighting her lamp, but she could not find the cap. Finally she gave it up. She extinguished her lamp and went back to bed. She fell asleep again, to be again awakened in the same fashion. That time she tore off the cap as before, but she did not fling it on the floor as before. Instead she held to it with a fierce grip. Her blood was up.

Holding fast to the white flimsy thing, she sprang out of bed, ran to the window which was open, slipped the screen, and flung it out; but a sudden gust of wind, though the night was calm, arose and it floated back in her face. She brushed it aside like a cobweb and she clutched at it. She was actually furious. It eluded her clutching fingers. Then she did not see it at all. She examined the floor, she lighted her lamp again and searched, but there was no sign of it.

Mrs. Simmons was then in such a rage that all terror had disappeared for the time. She did not know with what she was angry, but she had a sense of some mocking presence which was silently proving too strong against her weakness, and she was aroused to the utmost power of resistance. To be baffled like this and resisted by something which was as nothing to her straining senses filled her with intensest resentment.

Finally she got back into bed again; she did not go to sleep. She felt strangely drowsy, but she fought against it. She was wide awake, staring at the moonlight, when she suddenly felt the soft white strings of the thing tighten around her throat and realized that her enemy was again upon her. She seized the strings, untied them, twitched off the cap, ran with it to the table where her scissors lay and furiously cut it into small bits. She cut and tore, feeling an insane fury of gratification.

"There!" said she quite aloud. "I guess I sha'n't have any more trouble with this old cap."

She tossed the bits of muslin into a basket and went back to bed. Almost immediately she felt the soft strings tighten around her throat. Then at last she yielded, vanquished. This new refutal of all laws of reason by which she had learned, as it were, to spell her theory of life, was too much for her equilibrium. She pulled off the clinging strings feebly, drew the thing from her head, slid weakly out of bed, caught up her wrapper and hastened out of the room. She went noiselessly along the hall to her own old room: she entered, got into her familiar bed, and lay there the rest of the night shuddering and listening, and if she dozed, waking with a start at the feeling of the pressure upon her throat to find that it was not there, yet still to be unable to shake off entirely the horror.

When daylight came she crept back to the southwest chamber and hurriedly got some clothes in which to dress herself. It took all her resolution to enter the room, but nothing unusual happened while she was there. She hastened back to her old chamber, dressed herself and went down to breakfast with an imperturbable face. Her colour had not faded. When asked by Eliza Lippincott how she had slept, she replied with an appearance of calmness which was bewildering that she had not slept very well. She never did sleep very well in a new bed, and she thought she would go back to her old room.

Eliza Lippincott was not deceived, however, neither were the Gill sisters, nor the young girl, Flora. Eliza Lippineott spoke out bluntly.

"You needn't talk to me about sleeping well," said she. "I know something queer happened in that room last night by the way you act."

They all looked at Mrs. Simmons, inquiringly—the librarian with malicious curiosity and triumph, the minister with sad incredulity, Sophia Gill with fear and indignation, Amanda and the young girl with unmixed terror. The widow bore herself with dignity.

"I saw nothing nor heard nothing which I trust could not have been accounted for in some rational manner," said she.

"What was it?" persisted Eliza Lippincott.

"I do not wish to discuss the matter any further," replied Mrs. Simmons shortly. Then she passed her plate for more creamed potato. She felt that she would die before she confessed to the ghastly absurdity of that nightcap, or to having been disturbed by the flight of peacocks off a blue field of chintz after she had scoffed at the possibility of such a thing. She left the whole matter so vague that in a fashion she came off the mistress of the situation. She at all events impressed everybody by her coolness in the face of no one knew what nightly terror.

After breakfast, with the assistance of Amanda and Flora, she moved back into her old room. Scarcely a word was spoken during the process of moving, but they all worked with trembling haste and looked guilty when they met one another's eyes, as if conscious of betraying a common fear.

That afternoon the young minister, John Dunn, went to Sophia Gill and requested permission to occupy the southwest chamber that night.

"I don't ask to have my effects moved there," said he, "for I could scarcely afford a room so much superior to the one I now occupy, but I would like, if you please, to sleep there tonight for the purpose of refuting in my own person any unfortunate superstition which may have obtained root here."

Sophia Gill thanked the minister gratefully and eagerly accepted his offer.

"How anybody with common sense can believe for a minute in any such nonsense passes my comprehension," said she.

"It certainly passes mine how anybody with Christian faith can believe in ghosts," said the minister gently, and Sophia Gill felt a certain feminine contentment in hearing him. The minister was a child to her; she regarded him with no tincture of sentiment, and yet she loved to hear two other women covertly condemned by him and she herself thereby exalted.

That night about twelve o'clock the Reverend John Dunn essayed to go to his nightly slumber in the southwest chamber. He had been sitting up until that hour preparing his sermon.

He traversed the hall with a little night-lamp in his hand, opened the door of the southwest chamber, and essayed to enter. He might as well have essayed to enter the solid side of a house. He could not believe his senses. The door was certainly open; he could look into the room full of soft lights and shadows under the moonlight which streamed into the windows. He could see the bed in which he had expected to pass the night, but he could not enter. Whenever he strove to do so he had a curious sensation as if he were trying to press against an invisible person who met him with a force of opposition impossible to overcome. The minister was not an athletic man, yet he had considerable strength. He squared his elbows, set his mouth hard, and strove to push his way through into the room. The opposition which he met was as sternly and mutely terrible as the rocky fastness of a mountain in his way.

For a half hour John Dunn, doubting, raging, overwhelmed with spiritual agony as to the state of his own soul rather than fear, strove to enter that southwest chamber. He was simply powerless against this uncanny obstacle. Finally a great horror as of evil itself came over him. He was a nervous man and very young. He fairly fled to his own chamber and locked himself in like a terror-stricken girl.

The next morning he went to Miss Gill and told her frankly what had happened, and begged her to say nothing about it lest he should have injured the cause by the betrayal of such weakness, for he actually had come to believe that there was something wrong with the room.

"What it is I know not, Miss Sophia," said he, "but I firmly believe, against my will, that there is in that room some accursed evil power at work, of which modern faith and modern science know nothing."

Miss Sophia Gill listened with grimly lowering face. She had an inborn respect for the clergy, but she was bound to hold that southwest chamber in the dearly beloved old house of her fathers free of blame.

"I think I will sleep in that room myself tonight," she said, when the minister had finished.

He looked at her in doubt and dismay.

"I have great admiration for your faith and courage, Miss Sophia," he said, "but are you wise?"

"I am fully resolved to sleep in that room tonight," said she conclusively. There were occasions when Miss Sophia Gill could put on a manner of majesty, and she did now.

It was ten o'clock that night when Sophia Gill entered the southwest chamber. She had told her sister what she intended doing and had been proof against her tearful entreaties. Amanda was charged not to tell the young girl, Flora.

"There is no use in frightening that child over nothing," said Sophia.

Sophia, when she entered the southwest chamber, set the lamp which she carried on the bureau, and began moving about the rooms pulling down the curtains, taking off the nice white counterpane of the bed, and preparing generally for the night.

As she did so, moving with great coolness and deliberation, she became conscious that she was thinking some thoughts that were foreign to her. She began remembering what she could not have remembered, since she was not then born: the trouble over her mother's marriage, the bitter opposition, the shutting the door upon her, the ostracizing her from heart and home. She became aware of a most singular sensation as of bitter resentment herself, and not against the mother and sister who had so treated her own mother, but against her own mother, and then she became aware of a like bitterness extended to her own self. She felt malignant toward her mother as a young girl whom she remembered, though she could not have remembered, and she felt malignant toward her own self, and her sister Amanda, and Flora. Evil suggestions surged in her brain—suggestions which turned her heart to stone and which still fascinated her. And all the time by a sort of double consciousness she knew that what she thought was strange and not due to her own volition. She knew that she was thinking the thoughts of some other person, and she knew who. She felt herself possessed.

But there was tremendous strength in the woman's nature. She had inherited strength for good and righteous self-assertion, from the evil strength of her ancestors. They had turned their own weapons against themselves. She made an effort which seemed almost mortal, but was conscious that the hideous thing was gone from her. She thought her own thoughts. Then she scouted to herself the idea of anything supernatural about the terrific experience. "I am imagining everything," she told herself. She went on with her preparations; she went to the bureau to take down her hair. She looked in the glass and saw, instead of her softly parted waves of hair, harsh lines of iron-gray under the black borders of an old-fashioned head-dress. She saw instead of her smooth, broad forehead, a high one wrinkled with the intensest concentration of selfish reflections of a long life; she saw instead of her steady blue eyes, black ones with depths of malignant reserve, behind a broad meaning of ill will; she saw instead of her firm, benevolent mouth one with a hard, thin line, a network of melancholic wrinkles. She saw instead of her own face, middle-aged and good to see, the expression of a life of honesty and good will to others and patience under trials, the face of a very old woman scowling forever with unceasing hatred and misery at herself and all others, at life, and death, at that which had been and that which was to come. She saw instead of her own face in the glass, the face of her dead Aunt Harriet, topping her own shoulders in her own well-known dress!

Sophia Gill left the room. She went into the one which she shared with her sister Amanda. Amanda looked up and saw her standing there. She had set the lamp on a table, and she stood holding a handkerchief over her face. Amanda looked at her with terror.

"What is it? What is it, Sophia?" she gasped.

Sophia still stood with the handkerchief pressed to her face.

"Oh, Sophia, let me call somebody. Is your face hurt? Sophia, what is the matter with your face?" fairly shrieked Amanda.

Suddenly Sophia took the handkerchief from her face.

"Look at me, Amanda Gill," she said in an awful voice.

Amanda looked, shrinking.

"What is it? Oh, what is it? You don't look hurt. What is it, Sophia?"

"What do you see?"

"Why, I see you."

"Me?"

"Yes, you. What did you think I would see?"

Sophia Gill looked at her sister. "Never as long as I live will I tell you what I thought you would see, and you must never ask me," said she.

"Well, I never will, Sophia," replied Amanda, half weeping with terror.

"You won't try to sleep in that room again, Sophia?"

"No," said Sophia; "and I am going to sell this house."

THE VACANT LOT

When it became generally known in Townsend Centre that the Townsends were going to move to the city, there was great excitement and dismay. For the Townsends to move was about equivalent to the town's moving. The Townsend ancestors had founded the village a hundred years ago. The first Townsend had kept a wayside hostelry for man and beast, known as the "Sign of the Leopard." The sign-board, on which the leopard was painted a bright blue, was still extant, and prominently so, being nailed over the present Townsend's front door. This Townsend, by name David, kept the village store. There had been no tavern since the railroad was built through Townsend Centre in his father's day. Therefore the family, being ousted by the march of progress from their chosen employment, took up with a general country store as being the next thing to a country tavern, the principal difference consisting in the fact that all the guests were transients, never requiring bedchambers, securing their rest on the tops of sugar and flour barrels and codfish boxes, and their refreshment from stray nibblings at the stock in trade, to the profitless deplenishment of raisins and loaf sugar and crackers and cheese.

The flitting of the Townsends from the home of their ancestors was due to a sudden access of wealth from the death of a relative and the desire of Mrs. Townsend to secure better advantages for her son George, sixteen years old, in the way of education, and for her daughter Adrianna, ten years older, better matrimonial opportunities. However, this last inducement for leaving Townsend Centre was not openly stated, only ingeniously surmised by the neighbours.

"Sarah Townsend don't think there's anybody in Townsend Centre fit for her Adrianna to marry, and so she's goin' to take her to Boston to see if she can't pick up somebody there," they said. Then they wondered what Abel Lyons would do. He had been a humble suitor for Adrianna for years, but her mother had not approved, and Adrianna, who was dutiful, had repulsed him delicately and rather sadly. He was the only lover whom she had ever had, and she felt sorry and grateful; she was a plain, awkward girl, and had a patient recognition of the fact.

But her mother was ambitious, more so than her father, who was rather pugnaciously satisfied with what he had, and not easily disposed to change. However, he yielded to his wife and consented to sell out his business and purchase a house in Boston and move there.

David Townsend was curiously unlike the line of ancestors from whom he had come. He had either retrograded or advanced, as one might look at it. His moral character was certainly better, but he had not the fiery spirit and eager grasp at advantage which had distinguished them. Indeed, the old Townsends, though prominent and respected as men of property and influence, had reputations not above suspicions. There was more than one dark whisper regarding them handed down from mother to son in the village, and especially was this true of the first Townsend, he who built the tavern bearing the Sign of the Blue Leopard. His portrait, a hideous effort of contemporary art, hung in the garret of David Townsend's home. There was many a tale of wild roistering, if no worse, in that old roadhouse, and high stakes, and quarreling in cups, and blows, and money gotten in evil fashion, and the matter hushed up with a high hand for inquirers by the imperious Townsends who terrorized everybody. David Townsend terrorized nobody. He had gotten his little competence from his store by honest methods—the exchanging of sterling goods and true weights for country produce and country shillings. He was sober and reliable, with intense self-respect and a decided talent for the management of money. It was principally for this reason that he took great delight in his sudden wealth by legacy. He had thereby greater opportunities for the exercise of his native shrewdness in a bargain. This he evinced in his purchase of a house in Boston.

One day in spring the old Townsend house was shut up, the Blue Leopard was taken carefully down from his lair over the front door, the family chattels were loaded on the train, and the Townsends departed. It was a sad and eventful day for Townsend Centre. A man from Barre had rented the store—David had decided at the last not to sell—and the old familiars congregated in melancholy fashion and talked over the situation. An enormous pride over their departed townsman became evident. They paraded him, flaunting him like a banner in the eyes of the new man. "David is awful smart," they said; "there won't nobody get the better of him in the city if he has lived in Townsend Centre all his life. He's got his eyes open. Know what he paid for his house in Boston? Well, sir, that house cost twenty-five thousand dollars, and David he bought it for five. Yes, sir, he did."

"Must have been some out about it," remarked the new man, scowling over his counter. He was beginning to feel his disparaging situation.

"Not an out, sir. David he made sure on't. Catch him gettin' bit. Everythin' was in apple-pie order, hot an' cold water and all, and in one of the best locations of the city—real high-up street. David he said the rent in that street was never under a thousand. Yes, sir, David he got a bargain—five thousand dollars for a twenty-five-thousand-dollar house."

"Some out about it!" growled the new man over the counter.

However, as his fellow townsmen and allies stated, there seemed to be no doubt about the desirableness of the city house which David Townsend had purchased and the fact that he had secured it for an absurdly low price. The whole family were at first suspicious. It was ascertained that the house had cost a round sum only a few years ago; it was in perfect repair; nothing whatever was amiss with plumbing, furnace, anything. There was not even a soap factory within smelling distance, as Mrs. Townsend had vaguely surmised. She was sure that she had heard of houses being undesirable for such reasons, but there was no soap factory. They all sniffed and peeked; when the first rainfall came they looked at the ceiling, confidently expecting to see dark spots where the leaks had commenced, but there were none. They were forced to confess that their suspicions were allayed, that the house was perfect, even overshadowed with the mystery of a lower price than it was worth. That, however, was an additional perfection in the opinion of the Townsends, who had their share of New England thrift. They had lived just one month in their new house, and were happy, although at times somewhat lonely from missing the society of Townsend

Centre, when the trouble began. The Townsends, although they lived in a fine house in a genteel, almost fashionable, part of the city, were true to their antecedents and kept, as they had been accustomed, only one maid. She was the daughter of a farmer on the outskirts of their native village, was middle-aged, and had lived with them for the last ten years. One pleasant Monday morning she rose early and did the family washing before breakfast, which had been prepared by Mrs. Townsend and Adrianna, as was their habit on washing-days. The family were seated at the breakfast table in their basement dining-room, and this maid, whose name was Cordelia, was hanging out the clothes in the vacant lot. This vacant lot seemed a valuable one, being on a corner. It was rather singular that it had not been built upon. The Townsends had wondered at it and agreed that they would have preferred their own house to be there. They had, however, utilized it as far as possible with their innocent, rural disregard of property rights in unoccupied land.

"We might just as well hang out our washing in that vacant lot," Mrs. Townsend had told Cordelia the first Monday of their stay in the house. "Our little yard ain't half big enough for all our clothes, and it is sunnier there, too."

So Cordelia had hung out the wash there for four Mondays, and this was the fifth. The breakfast was about half finished—they had reached the buckwheat cakes—when this maid came rushing into the dining-room and stood regarding them, speechless, with a countenance indicative of the utmost horror. She was deadly pale. Her hands, sodden with soapsuds, hung twitching at her sides in the folds of her calico gown; her very hair, which was light and sparse, seemed to bristle with fear. All the Townsends turned and looked at her. David and George rose with a half-defined idea of burglars.

"Cordelia Battles, what is the matter?" cried Mrs. Townsend. Adrianna gasped for breath and turned as white as the maid. "What is the matter?" repeated Mrs. Townsend, but the maid was unable to speak. Mrs. Townsend, who could be peremptory, sprang up, ran to the frightened woman and shook her violently. "Cordelia Battles, you speak," said she, "and not stand there staring that way, as if you were struck dumb! What is the matter with you?"

Then Cordelia spoke in a fainting voice.

"There's—somebody else—hanging out clothes—in the vacant lot," she gasped, and clutched at a chair for support.

"Who?" cried Mrs. Townsend, rousing to indignation, for already she had assumed a proprietorship in the vacant lot. "Is it the folks in the next house? I'd like to know what right they have! We are next to that vacant lot."

"I—dunno—who it is," gasped Cordelia. "Why, we've seen that girl next door go to mass every morning," said Mrs. Townsend. "She's got a fiery red head. Seems as if you might know her by this time, Cordelia."

"It ain't that girl," gasped Cordelia. Then she added in a horror-stricken voice, "I couldn't see who 'twas."

They all stared.

"Why couldn't you see?" demanded her mistress. "Are you struck blind?"

"No, ma'am."

"Then why couldn't you see?"

"All I could see was—" Cordelia hesitated, with an expression of the utmost horror.

"Go on," said Mrs. Townsend, impatiently.

"All I could see was the shadow of somebody, very slim, hanging out the clothes, and—"

"What?"

"I could see the shadows of the things flappin' on their line."

"You couldn't see the clothes?"

"Only the shadow on the ground."

"What kind of clothes were they?"

"Queer," replied Cordelia, with a shudder.

"If I didn't know you so well, I should think you had been drinking," said Mrs. Townsend. "Now, Cordelia Battles, I'm going out in that vacant lot and see myself what you're talking about."

"I can't go," gasped the woman.

With that Mrs. Townsend and all the others, except Adrianna, who remained to tremble with the maid, sallied forth into the vacant lot. They had to go out the area gate into the street to reach it. It was nothing unusual in the way of vacant lots. One large poplar tree, the relic of the old forest which had once flourished there, twinkled in one corner; for the rest, it was overgrown with coarse weeds and a few dusty flowers. The Townsends stood just inside the rude board fence which divided the lot from the street and stared with wonder and horror, for Cordelia had told the truth. They all saw what she had described—the shadow of an exceedingly slim woman moving along the ground with up-stretched arms, the shadows of strange, nondescript garments flapping from a shadowy line, but when they looked up for the substance of the shadows nothing was to be seen except the clear, blue October air.

"My goodness!" gasped Mrs. Townsend. Her face assumed a strange gathering of wrath in the midst of her terror. Suddenly she made a determined move forward, although her husband strove to hold her back.

"You let me be," said she. She moved forward. Then she recoiled and gave a loud shriek. "The wet sheet flapped in my face," she cried. "Take me away, take me away!" Then she fainted. Between them they got her back to the house. "It was awful," she moaned when she came to herself, with the family all around her where she lay on the dining-room floor. "Oh, David, what do you suppose it is?"

"Nothing at all," replied David Townsend stoutly. He was remarkable for courage and staunch belief in actualities. He was now denying to himself that he had seen anything unusual.

"Oh, there was," moaned his wife.

"I saw something," said George, in a sullen, boyish bass.

The maid sobbed convulsively and so did Adrianna for sympathy.

"We won't talk any about it," said David. "Here, Jane, you drink this hot tea—it will do you good; and Cordelia, you hang out the clothes in our own yard. George, you go and put up the line for her."

"The line is out there," said George, with a jerk of his shoulder.

"Are you afraid?"

"No, I ain't," replied the boy resentfully, and went out with a pale face.

After that Cordelia hung the Townsend wash in the yard of their own house, standing always with her back to the vacant lot. As for David Townsend, he spent a good deal of his time in the lot watching the shadows, but he came to no explanation, although he strove to satisfy himself with many.

"I guess the shadows come from the smoke from our chimneys, or else the poplar tree," he said.

"Why do the shadows come on Monday mornings, and no other?" demanded his wife.

David was silent.

Very soon new mysteries arose. One day Cordelia rang the dinner-bell at their usual dinner hour, the same as in Townsend Centre, high noon, and the family assembled. With amazement Adrianna looked at the dishes on the table.

"Why, that's queer!" she said.

"What's queer?" asked her mother.

Cordelia stopped short as she was about setting a tumbler of water beside a plate, and the water slopped over.

"Why," said Adrianna, her face paling, "I—thought there was boiled dinner. I—smelt cabbage cooking."

"I knew there would something else come up," gasped Cordelia, leaning hard on the back of Adrianna's chair.

"What do you mean?" asked Mrs. Townsend sharply, but her own face began to assume the shocked pallour which it was so easy nowadays for all their faces to assume at the merest suggestion of anything out of the common.

"I smelt cabbage cooking all the morning up in my room," Adrianna said faintly, "and here's codfish and potatoes for dinner."

The Townsends all looked at one another. David rose with an exclamation and rushed out of the room. The others waited tremblingly. When he came back his face was lowering.

"What did you—" Mrs. Townsend asked hesitatingly.

"There's some smell of cabbage out there," he admitted reluctantly. Then he looked at her with a challenge. "It comes from the next house," he said. "Blows over our house."

"Our house is higher."

"I don't care; you can never account for such things."

"Cordelia," said Mrs. Townsend, "you go over to the next house and you ask if they've got cabbage for dinner."

Cordelia switched out of the room, her mouth set hard. She came back promptly.

"Says they never have cabbage," she announced with gloomy triumph and a conclusive glance at Mr. Townsend. "Their girl was real sassy."

"Oh, father, let's move away; let's sell the house," cried Adrianna in a panic-stricken tone.

"If you think I'm going to sell a house that I got as cheap as this one because we smell cabbage in a vacant lot, you're mistaken," replied David firmly.

"It isn't the cabbage alone," said Mrs. Townsend.

"And a few shadows," added David. "I am tired of such nonsense. I thought you had more sense, Jane."

"One of the boys at school asked me if we lived in the house next to the vacant lot on Wells Street and whistled when I said 'Yes,'" remarked George.

"Let him whistle," said Mr. Townsend.

After a few hours the family, stimulated by Mr. Townsend's calm, common sense, agreed that it was exceedingly foolish to be disturbed by a mysterious odour of cabbage. They even laughed at themselves.

"I suppose we have got so nervous over those shadows hanging out clothes that we notice every little thing," conceded Mrs. Townsend.

"You will find out some day that that is no more to be regarded than the cabbage," said her husband.

"You can't account for that wet sheet hitting my face," said Mrs. Townsend, doubtfully.

"You imagined it."

"I FELT it."

That afternoon things went on as usual in the household until nearly four o'clock. Adrianna went downtown to do some shopping. Mrs. Townsend sat sewing beside the bay window in her room, which was a front one in the third story. George had not got home. Mr. Townsend was writing a letter in the library. Cordelia was busy in the basement; the twilight, which was coming earlier and earlier every night, was beginning to gather, when suddenly there was a loud crash which shook the house from its foundations. Even the dishes on the sideboard rattled, and the glasses rang like bells. The pictures on the walls of Mrs. Townsend's room swung out from the walls. But that was not all: every looking-glass in the house cracked simultaneously—as nearly as they could judge— from top to bottom, then shivered into fragments over the floors. Mrs. Townsend was too frightened to scream. She sat huddled in her chair, gasping for breath, her eyes, rolling from side to side in incredulous terror, turned toward the street. She saw a great black group of people crossing it just in front of the vacant lot. There was something inexpressibly strange and gloomy about this moving group; there was an effect of sweeping, wavings and foldings of sable draperies and gleams of deadly white faces; then they passed. She twisted her head to see, and they disappeared in the vacant lot. Mr. Townsend came hurrying into the room; he was pale, and looked at once angry and alarmed.

"Did you fall?" he asked inconsequently, as if his wife, who was small, could have produced such a manifestation by a fall.

"Oh, David, what is it?" whispered Mrs. Townsend.

"Darned if I know!" said David.

"Don't swear. It's too awful. Oh, see the looking-glass, David!"

"I see it. The one over the library mantel is broken, too."

"Oh, it is a sign of death!"

Cordelia's feet were heard as she staggered on the stairs. She almost fell into the room. She reeled over to Mr. Townsend and clutched his arm. He cast a sidewise glance, half furious, half commiserating at her.

"Well, what is it all about?" he asked.

"I don't know. What is it? Oh, what is it? The looking-glass in the kitchen is broken. All over the floor. Oh, oh! What is it?"

"I don't know any more than you do. I didn't do it."

"Lookin'-glasses broken is a sign of death in the house," said Cordelia. "If it's me, I hope I'm ready; but I'd rather die than be so scared as I've been lately."

Mr. Townsend shook himself loose and eyed the two trembling women with gathering resolution.

"Now, look here, both of you," he said. "This is nonsense. You'll die sure enough of fright if you keep on this way. I was a fool myself to be startled. Everything it is is an earthquake."

"Oh, David!" gasped his wife, not much reassured.

"It is nothing but an earthquake," persisted Mr. Townsend. "It acted just like that. Things always are broken on the walls, and the middle of the room isn't affected. I've read about it."

Suddenly Mrs. Townsend gave a loud shriek and pointed.

"How do you account for that," she cried, "if it's an earthquake? Oh, oh, oh!"

She was on the verge of hysterics. Her husband held her firmly by the arm as his eyes followed the direction of her rigid pointing finger. Cordelia looked also, her eyes seeming converged to a bright point of fear. On the floor in front of the broken looking-glass lay a mass of black stuff in a grewsome long ridge.

"It's something you dropped there," almost shouted Mr. Townsend.

"It ain't. Oh!"

Mr. Townsend dropped his wife's arm and took one stride toward the object. It was a very long crape veil. He lifted it, and it floated out from his arm as if imbued with electricity.

"It's yours," he said to his wife.

"Oh, David, I never had one. You know, oh, you know I—shouldn't—unless you died. How came it there?"

"I'm darned if I know," said David, regarding it. He was deadly pale, but still resentful rather than afraid.

"Don't hold it; don't!"

"I'd like to know what in thunder all this means?" said David. He gave the thing an angry toss and it fell on the floor in exactly the same long heap as before.

Cordelia began to weep with racking sobs. Mrs. Townsend reached out and caught her husband's hand, clutching it hard with ice-cold fingers.

"What's got into this house, anyhow?" he growled.

"You'll have to sell it. Oh, David, we can't live here."

"As for my selling a house I paid only five thousand for when it's worth twenty-five, for any such nonsense as this, I won't!"

David gave one stride toward the black veil, but it rose from the floor and moved away before him across the room at exactly the same height as if suspended from a woman's head. He pursued it, clutching vainly, all around the room, then he swung himself on his heel with an exclamation and the thing fell to the floor again in the long heap. Then were heard hurrying feet on the stairs and Adrianna burst into the room. She ran straight to her father and clutched his arm; she tried to speak, but she chattered unintelligibly; her face was blue. Her father shook her violently.

"Adrianna, do have more sense!" he cried.

"Oh, David, how can you talk so?" sobbed her mother.

"I can't help it. I'm mad!" said he with emphasis. "What has got into this house and you all, anyhow?"

"What is it, Adrianna, poor child," asked her mother. "Only look what has happened here."

"It's an earthquake," said her father staunchly; "nothing to be afraid of."

"How do you account for THAT?" said Mrs. Townsend in an awful voice, pointing to the veil.

Adrianna did not look—she was too engrossed with her own terrors. She began to speak in a breathless voice.

"I—was—coming—by the vacant lot," she panted, "and—I—I—had my new hat in a paper bag and—a parcel of blue ribbon, and—I saw a crowd, an awful—oh! a whole crowd of people with white faces, as if—they were dressed all in black."

"Where are they now?"

"I don't know. Oh!" Adrianna sank gasping feebly into a chair.

"Get her some water, David," sobbed her mother.

David rushed with an impatient exclamation out of the room and returned with a glass of water which he held to his daughter's lips.

"Here, drink this!" he said roughly.

"Oh, David, how can you speak so?" sobbed his wife.

"I can't help it. I'm mad clean through," said David.

Then there was a hard bound upstairs, and George entered. He was very white, but he grinned at them with an appearance of unconcern.

"Hullo!" he said in a shaking voice, which he tried to control. "What on earth's to pay in that vacant lot now?"

"Well, what is it?" demanded his father.

"Oh, nothing, only—well, there are lights over it exactly as if there was a house there, just about where the windows would be. It looked as if you could walk right in, but when you look close there are those old dried-up weeds rattling away on the ground the same as ever. I looked at it and couldn't believe my eyes. A woman saw it, too. She came along just as I did. She gave one look, then she screeched and ran. I waited for some one else, but nobody came."

Mr. Townsend rushed out of the room.

"I daresay it'll be gone when he gets there," began George, then he stared round the room. "What's to pay here?" he cried.

"Oh, George, the whole house shook all at once, and all the looking-glasses broke," wailed his mother, and Adrianna and Cordelia joined.

George whistled with pale lips. Then Mr. Townsend entered.

"Well," asked George, "see anything?"

"I don't want to talk," said his father. "I've stood just about enough."

"We've got to sell out and go back to Townsend Centre," cried his wife in a wild voice. "Oh, David, say you'll go back."

"I won't go back for any such nonsense as this, and sell a twenty-five thousand dollar house for five thousand," said he firmly.

But that very night his resolution was shaken. The whole family watched together in the dining-room. They were all afraid to go to bed—that is, all except possibly Mr. Townsend. Mrs. Townsend declared firmly that she for one would leave that awful house and go back to Townsend Centre whether he came or not, unless they all stayed together and watched, and Mr. Townsend yielded. They chose the dining-room for the reason that it was nearer the street should they wish to make their egress hurriedly, and they took up their station around the dining-table on which Cordelia had placed a luncheon.

"It looks exactly as if we were watching with a corpse," she said in a horror-stricken whisper.

"Hold your tongue if you can't talk sense," said Mr. Townsend.

The dining-room was very large, finished in oak, with a dark blue paper above the wainscotting. The old sign of the tavern, the Blue Leopard, hung over the mantel-shelf. Mr. Townsend had insisted on hanging it there. He had a curious pride in it. The family sat together until after midnight and nothing unusual happened. Mrs. Townsend began to nod; Mr. Townsend read the paper ostentatiously. Adrianna and Cordelia stared with roving eyes about the room, then at each other as if comparing notes on terror. George had a book which he studied furtively. All at once Adrianna gave a startled exclamation and Cordelia echoed her. George whistled faintly. Mrs. Townsend awoke with a start and Mr. Townsend's paper rattled to the floor.

"Look!" gasped Adrianna.

The sign of the Blue Leopard over the shelf glowed as if a lantern hung over it. The radiance was thrown from above. It grew brighter and brighter as they watched. The Blue Leopard seemed to crouch and spring with life. Then the door into the front hall opened—the outer door, which had been carefully locked. It squeaked and they all recognized it. They sat staring. Mr. Townsend was as transfixed as the rest. They heard the outer door shut, then the door into the room swung open and slowly that awful black group of people which they had seen in the afternoon entered. The Townsends with one accord rose and huddled together in a far corner; they all held to each other and stared. The people, their faces gleaming with a whiteness of death, their black robes waving and folding, crossed the room. They were a trifle above mortal height, or seemed so to the terrified eyes which saw them. They reached the mantel-shelf where the sign-board hung, then a black-draped long arm was seen to rise and make a motion, as if plying a knocker. Then the whole company passed out of sight, as if through the wall, and the room was as before. Mrs. Townsend was shaking in a nervous chill, Adrianna was almost fainting, Cordelia was in hysterics. David Townsend stood glaring in a curious way at the sign of the Blue Leopard. George stared at him with a look of horror. There was something in his father's face which made him forget everything else. At last he touched his arm timidly.

"Father," he whispered.

David turned and regarded him with a look of rage and fury, then his face cleared; he passed his hand over his forehead.

"Good Lord! What DID come to me?" he muttered.

"You looked like that awful picture of old Tom Townsend in the garret in Townsend Centre, father," whimpered the boy, shuddering.

"Should think I might look like 'most any old cuss after such darned work as this," growled David, but his face was white. "Go and pour out some hot tea for your mother," he ordered the boy sharply. He himself shook Cordelia violently. "Stop such actions!" he shouted in her ears, and shook her again. "Ain't you a church member?" he demanded; "what be you afraid of? You ain't done nothin' wrong, have ye?"

Then Cordelia quoted Scripture in a burst of sobs and laughter.

"Behold, I was shapen in iniquity; and in sin did my mother conceive me," she cried out. "If I ain't done wrong, mebbe them that's come before me did, and when the Evil One and the Powers of Darkness is abroad I'm liable, I'm liable!" Then she laughed loud and long and shrill.

"If you don't hush up," said David, but still with that white terror and horror on his own face, "I'll bundle you out in that vacant lot whether or no. I mean it."

Then Cordelia was quiet, after one wild roll of her eyes at him. The colour was returning to Adrianna's cheeks; her mother was drinking hot tea in spasmodic gulps.

"It's after midnight," she gasped, "and I don't believe they'll come again tonight. Do you, David?"

"No, I don't," said David conclusively.

"Oh, David, we mustn't stay another night in this awful house."

"We won't. Tomorrow we'll pack off bag and baggage to Townsend Centre, if it takes all the fire department to move us," said David.

Adrianna smiled in the midst of her terror. She thought of Abel Lyons.

The next day Mr. Townsend went to the real estate agent who had sold him the house.

"It's no use," he said, "I can't stand it. Sell the house for what you can get. I'll give it away rather than keep it."

Then he added a few strong words as to his opinion of parties who sold him such an establishment. But the agent pleaded innocent for the most part.

"I'll own I suspected something wrong when the owner, who pledged me to secrecy as to his name, told me to sell that place for what I could get, and did not limit me. I had never heard anything, but I began to suspect something was wrong. Then I made a few inquiries and found out that there was a rumour in the neighbourhood that there was something out of the usual about that vacant lot. I had wondered myself why it wasn't built upon. There was a story about it's being undertaken once, and the contract made, and the contractor dying; then another man took it and one of the workmen was killed on his way to dig the cellar, and the others struck. I didn't pay much attention to it. I never believed much in that sort of thing anyhow, and then, too, I couldn't find out that there had ever been anything wrong about the house itself, except as the people who had lived there were said to have seen and heard queer things in the vacant lot, so I thought you might be able to get along, especially as you didn't look like a man who was timid, and the house was such a bargain as I never handled before. But this you tell me is beyond belief."

"Do you know the names of the people who formerly owned the vacant lot?" asked Mr. Townsend.

"I don't know for certain," replied the agent, "for the original owners flourished long before your or my day, but I do know that the lot goes by the name of the old Gaston lot. What's the matter? Are you ill?"

"No; it is nothing," replied Mr. Townsend. "Get what you can for the house; perhaps another family might not be as troubled as we have been."

"I hope you are not going to leave the city?" said the agent, urbanely.

"I am going back to Townsend Centre as fast as steam can carry me after we get packed up and out of that cursed house," replied Mr. David Townsend.

He did not tell the agent nor any of his family what had caused him to start when told the name of the former owners of the lot. He remembered all at once the story of a ghastly murder which had taken place in the Blue Leopard. The victim's name was Gaston and the murderer had never been discovered.

THE LOST GHOST

Mrs. John Emerson, sitting with her needlework beside the window, looked out and saw Mrs. Rhoda Meserve coming down the street, and knew at once by the trend of her steps and the cant of her head that she meditated turning in at her gate. She also knew by a certain something about her general carriage—a thrusting forward of the neck, a bustling hitch of the shoulders—that she had important news. Rhoda Meserve always had the news as soon as the news was in being, and generally Mrs. John Emerson was the first to whom she imparted it. The two women had been friends ever since Mrs. Meserve had married Simon Meserve and come to the village to live.

Mrs. Meserve was a pretty woman, moving with graceful flirts of ruffling skirts; her clear-cut, nervous face, as delicately tinted as a shell, looked brightly from the plumy brim of a black hat at Mrs. Emerson in the window. Mrs. Emerson was glad to see her coming. She returned the greeting with enthusiasm, then rose hurriedly, ran into the cold parlour and brought out one of the best rocking-chairs. She was just in time, after drawing it up beside the opposite window, to greet her friend at the door.

"Good-afternoon," said she. "I declare, I'm real glad to see you. I've been alone all day. John went to the city this morning. I thought of coming over to your house this afternoon, but I couldn't bring my sewing very well. I am putting the ruffles on my new black dress skirt."

"Well, I didn't have a thing on hand except my crochet work," responded Mrs. Meserve, "and I thought I'd just run over a few minutes."

"I'm real glad you did," repeated Mrs. Emerson. "Take your things right off. Here, I'll put them on my bed in the bedroom. Take the rocking-chair."

Mrs. Meserve settled herself in the parlour rocking-chair, while Mrs. Emerson carried her shawl and hat into the little adjoining bedroom. When she returned Mrs. Meserve was rocking peacefully and was already at work hooking blue wool in and out.

"That's real pretty," said Mrs. Emerson.

"Yes, I think it's pretty," replied Mrs. Meserve.

"I suppose it's for the church fair?"

"Yes. I don't suppose it'll bring enough to pay for the worsted, let alone the work, but I suppose I've got to make something."

"How much did that one you made for the fair last year bring?"

"Twenty-five cents."

"It's wicked, ain't it?"

"I rather guess it is. It takes me a week every minute I can get to make one. I wish those that bought such things for twenty-five cents had to make them. Guess they'd sing another song. Well, I suppose I oughtn't to complain as long as it is for the Lord, but sometimes it does seem as if the Lord didn't get much out of it."

"Well, it's pretty work," said Mrs. Emerson, sitting down at the opposite window and taking up her dress skirt.

"Yes, it is real pretty work. I just LOVE to crochet."

The two women rocked and sewed and crocheted in silence for two or three minutes. They were both waiting. Mrs. Meserve waited for the other's curiosity to develop in order that her news might have, as it were, a befitting stage entrance. Mrs. Emerson waited for the news. Finally she could wait no longer.

"Well, what's the news?" said she.

"Well, I don't know as there's anything very particular," hedged the other woman, prolonging the situation.

"Yes, there is; you can't cheat me," replied Mrs. Emerson.

"Now, how do you know?"

"By the way you look."

Mrs. Meserve laughed consciously and rather vainly.

"Well, Simon says my face is so expressive I can't hide anything more than five minutes no matter how hard I try," said she. "Well, there is some news. Simon came home with it this noon. He heard it in South Dayton. He had some business over there this morning. The old Sargent place is let."

Mrs. Emerson dropped her sewing and stared.

"You don't say so!"

"Yes, it is."

"Who to?"

"Why, some folks from Boston that moved to South Dayton last year. They haven't been satisfied with the house they had there—it wasn't large enough. The man has got considerable property and can afford to live pretty well. He's got a wife and his unmarried sister in the family. The sister's got money, too. He does business in Boston and it's just as easy to get to Boston from here as from South Dayton, and so they're coming here. You know the old Sargent house is a splendid place."

"Yes, it's the handsomest house in town, but—"

"Oh, Simon said they told him about that and he just laughed. Said he wasn't afraid and neither was his wife and sister. Said he'd risk ghosts rather than little tucked-up sleeping-rooms without any sun, like they've had in the Dayton house. Said he'd rather risk SEEING ghosts, than risk being ghosts themselves. Simon said they said he was a great hand to joke."

"Oh, well," said Mrs. Emerson, "it is a beautiful house, and maybe there isn't anything in those stories. It never seemed to me they came very straight anyway. I never took much stock in them. All I thought was—if his wife was nervous."

"Nothing in creation would hire me to go into a house that I'd ever heard a word against of that kind," declared Mrs. Meserve with emphasis. "I wouldn't go into that house if they would give me the rent. I've seen enough of haunted houses to last me as long as I live."

Mrs. Emerson's face acquired the expression of a hunting hound.

"Have you?" she asked in an intense whisper.

"Yes, I have. I don't want any more of it."

"Before you came here?"

"Yes; before I was married—when I was quite a girl."

Mrs. Meserve had not married young. Mrs. Emerson had mental calculations when she heard that.

"Did you really live in a house that was—" she whispered fearfully.

Mrs. Meserve nodded solemnly.

"Did you really ever—see—anything—"

Mrs. Meserve nodded.

"You didn't see anything that did you any harm?"

"No, I didn't see anything that did me harm looking at it in one way, but it don't do anybody in this world any good to see things that haven't any business to be seen in it. You never get over it."

There was a moment's silence. Mrs. Emerson's features seemed to sharpen.

"Well, of course I don't want to urge you," said she, "if you don't feel like talking about it; but maybe it might do you good to tell it out, if it's on your mind, worrying you."

"I try to put it out of my mind," said Mrs. Meserve.

"Well, it's just as you feel."

"I never told anybody but Simon," said Mrs. Meserve. "I never felt as if it was wise perhaps. I didn't know what folks might think. So many don't believe in anything they can't understand, that they might think my mind wasn't right. Simon advised me not to talk about it. He said he didn't believe it was anything supernatural, but he had to own up that he couldn't give any explanation for it to save his life. He had to own up that he didn't believe anybody could. Then he said he wouldn't talk about it. He said lots of folks would sooner tell folks my head wasn't right than to own up they couldn't see through it."

"I'm sure I wouldn't say so," returned Mrs. Emerson reproachfully. "You know better than that, I hope."

"Yes, I do," replied Mrs. Meserve. "I know you wouldn't say so."

"And I wouldn't tell it to a soul if you didn't want me to."

"Well, I'd rather you wouldn't."

"I won't speak of it even to Mr. Emerson."

"I'd rather you wouldn't even to him."

"I won't."

Mrs. Emerson took up her dress skirt again; Mrs. Meserve hooked up another loop of blue wool. Then she begun:

"Of course," said she, "I ain't going to say positively that I believe or disbelieve in ghosts, but all I tell you is what I saw. I can't explain it. I don't pretend I can, for I can't. If you can, well and good; I shall be glad, for it will stop tormenting me as it has done and always will otherwise. There hasn't been a day nor a night since it happened that I haven't thought of it, and always I have felt the shivers go down my back when I did."

"That's an awful feeling," Mrs. Emerson said.

"Ain't it? Well, it happened before I was married, when I was a girl and lived in East Wilmington. It was the first year I lived there. You know my family all died five years before that. I told you."

Mrs. Emerson nodded.

"Well, I went there to teach school, and I went to board with a Mrs. Amelia Dennison and her sister, Mrs. Bird. Abby, her name was—Abby Bird. She was a widow; she had never had any children. She had a little money—Mrs. Dennison didn't have any—and she had come to East Wilmington and bought the house they lived in. It was a real pretty house, though it was very old and run down. It had cost Mrs. Bird a good deal to put it in order. I guess that was the reason they took me to board. I guess they thought it would help along a little. I guess what I paid for my board about kept us all in victuals. Mrs. Bird had enough to live on if they were careful, but she had spent so much fixing up the old house that they must have been a little pinched for awhile.

"Anyhow, they took me to board, and I thought I was pretty lucky to get in there. I had a nice room, big and sunny and furnished pretty, the paper and paint all new, and everything as neat as wax. Mrs. Dennison was one of the best cooks I ever saw, and I had a little stove in my room, and there was always a nice fire there when I got home from school. I thought I hadn't been in such a nice place since I lost my own home, until I had been there about three weeks.

"I had been there about three weeks before I found it out, though I guess it had been going on ever since they had been in the house, and that was most four months. They hadn't said anything about it, and I didn't wonder, for there they had just bought the house and been to so much expense and trouble fixing it up.

"Well, I went there in September. I begun my school the first Monday. I remember it was a real cold fall, there was a frost the middle of September, and I had to put on my winter coat. I remember when I came home that night (let me see, I began school on a Monday, and that was two weeks from the next Thursday), I took off my coat downstairs and laid it on the table in the front entry. It was a real nice coat—heavy black broadcloth trimmed with fur; I had had it the winter before. Mrs. Bird called after me as I went upstairs that I ought not to leave it in the front entry for fear somebody might come in and take it, but I only laughed and called back to her that I wasn't afraid. I never was much afraid of burglars.

"Well, though it was hardly the middle of September, it was a real cold night. I remember my room faced west, and the sun was getting low, and the sky was a pale yellow and purple, just as you see it sometimes in the winter when there is going to be a cold snap. I rather think that was the night the frost came the first time. I know Mrs. Dennison covered up some flowers she had in the front yard, anyhow. I remember looking out and seeing an old green plaid shawl of hers over the verbena bed. There was a fire in my little wood-stove. Mrs. Bird made it, I know. She was a real motherly sort of woman; she always seemed to be the happiest when she was doing something to make other folks happy and comfortable. Mrs. Dennison told me she had always been so. She said she had coddled her husband within an inch of his life. 'It's lucky Abby never had any children,' she said, 'for she would have spoilt them.'

"Well, that night I sat down beside my nice little fire and ate an apple. There was a plate of nice apples on my table. Mrs. Bird put them there. I was always very fond of apples. Well, I sat down and ate an apple, and was having a beautiful time, and thinking how lucky I was to have got board in such a place with such nice folks, when I heard a queer little sound at my door. It was such a little hesitating sort of sound that it sounded more like a fumble than a knock, as if some one very timid, with very little hands, was feeling along the door, not quite daring to knock. For a minute I thought it was a mouse. But I waited and it came again, and then I made up my mind it was a knock, but a very little scared one, so I said, 'Come in.'

"But nobody came in, and then presently I heard the knock again. Then I got up and opened the door, thinking it was very queer, and I had a frightened feeling without knowing why.

"Well, I opened the door, and the first thing I noticed was a draught of cold air, as if the front door downstairs was open, but there was a strange close smell about the cold draught. It smelled more like a cellar that had been shut up for years, than out-of-doors. Then I saw something. I saw my coat first. The thing that held it was so small that I couldn't see much of anything else. Then I saw a little white face with eyes so scared and wishful that they seemed as if they might eat a hole in anybody's heart. It was a dreadful little face, with something about it which made it different from any other face on earth, but it was so pitiful that somehow it did away a good deal with the dreadfulness. And there were two little hands spotted purple with the cold, holding up my winter coat, and a strange little far-away voice said: 'I can't find my mother.'

"'For Heaven's sake,' I said, 'who are you?'

"Then the little voice said again: 'I can't find my mother.'

"All the time I could smell the cold and I saw that it was about the child; that cold was clinging to her as if she had come out of some deadly cold place. Well, I took my coat, I did not know what else to do, and the cold was clinging to that. It was as cold as if it had come off ice. When I had the coat I could see the child more plainly. She was dressed in one little white garment made very simply. It was a nightgown, only very long, quite covering her feet, and I could see dimly through it her little thin body mottled purple with the cold. Her face did not look so cold; that was a clear waxen white. Her hair was dark, but it looked as if it might be dark only because it was so damp, almost wet, and might really be light hair. It clung very close to her forehead, which was round and white. She would have been very beautiful if she had not been so dreadful.

"'Who are you?' says I again, looking at her.

"She looked at me with her terrible pleading eyes and did not say anything.

"'What are you?' says I. Then she went away. She did not seem to run or walk like other children. She flitted, like one of those little filmy white butterflies, that don't seem like real ones they are so light, and move as if they had no weight. But she looked back from the head of the stairs. 'I can't find my mother,' said she, and I never heard such a voice.

"'Who is your mother?' says I, but she was gone.

"Well, I thought for a moment I should faint away. The room got dark and I heard a singing in my ears. Then I flung my coat onto the bed. My hands were as cold as ice from holding it, and I stood in my door, and called first Mrs. Bird and then Mrs. Dennison. I didn't dare go down over the stairs where that had gone. It seemed to me I should go mad if I didn't see somebody or something like other folks on the face of the earth. I thought I should never make anybody hear, but I could hear them stepping about downstairs, and I could smell biscuits baking for supper. Somehow the smell of those biscuits seemed the only natural thing left to keep me in my right mind. I didn't dare go over those stairs. I just stood there and called, and finally I heard the entry door open and Mrs. Bird called back:

"'What is it? Did you call, Miss Arms?'

"'Come up here; come up here as quick as you can, both of you,' I screamed out; 'quick, quick, quick!'

"I heard Mrs. Bird tell Mrs. Dennison: 'Come quick, Amelia, something is the matter in Miss Arms' room.' It struck me even then that she expressed herself rather queerly, and it struck me as very queer, indeed, when they both got upstairs and I saw that they knew what had happened, or that they knew of what nature the happening was.

"'What is it, dear?' asked Mrs. Bird, and her pretty, loving voice had a strained sound. I saw her look at Mrs. Dennison and I saw Mrs. Dennison look back at her.

"'For God's sake,' says I, and I never spoke so before—'for God's sake, what was it brought my coat upstairs?'

"'What was it like?' asked Mrs. Dennison in a sort of failing voice, and she looked at her sister again and her sister looked back at her.

"'It was a child I have never seen here before. It looked like a child,' says I, 'but I never saw a child so dreadful, and it had on a nightgown, and said she couldn't find her mother. Who was it? What was it?'

"I thought for a minute Mrs. Dennison was going to faint, but Mrs. Bird hung onto her and rubbed her hands, and whispered in her ear (she had the cooingest kind of voice), and I ran and got her a glass of cold water. I tell you it took considerable courage to go downstairs alone, but they had set a lamp on the entry table so I could see. I don't believe I could have spunked up enough to have gone downstairs in the dark, thinking every second that child might be close to me. The lamp and the smell of the biscuits baking seemed to sort of keep my courage up, but I tell you I didn't waste much time going down those stairs and out into the kitchen for a glass of water. I pumped as if the house was afire, and I grabbed the first thing I came across in the shape of a tumbler: it was a painted one that Mrs. Dennison's Sunday school class gave her, and it was meant for a flower vase.

"Well, I filled it and then ran upstairs. I felt every minute as if something would catch my feet, and I held the glass to Mrs. Dennison's lips, while Mrs. Bird held her head up, and she took a good long swallow, then she looked hard at the tumbler.

"'Yes,' says I, 'I know I got this one, but I took the first I came across, and it isn't hurt a mite.'

"'Don't get the painted flowers wet,' says Mrs. Dennison very feebly, 'they'll wash off if you do.'

"'I'll be real careful,' says I. I knew she set a sight by that painted tumbler.

"The water seemed to do Mrs. Dennison good, for presently she pushed Mrs. Bird away and sat up. She had been laying down on my bed.

"'I'm all over it now,' says she, but she was terribly white, and her eyes looked as if they saw something outside things. Mrs. Bird wasn't much better, but she always had a sort of settled sweet, good look that nothing could disturb to any great extent. I knew I looked dreadful, for I caught a glimpse of myself in the glass, and I would hardly have known who it was.

"Mrs. Dennison, she slid off the bed and walked sort of tottery to a chair. 'I was silly to give way so,' says she.

"'No, you wasn't silly, sister,' says Mrs. Bird. 'I don't know what this means any more than you do, but whatever it is, no one ought to be called silly for being overcome by anything so different from other things which we have known all our lives.'

"Mrs. Dennison looked at her sister, then she looked at me, then back at her sister again, and Mrs. Bird spoke as if she had been asked a question.

"'Yes,' says she, 'I do think Miss Arms ought to be told—that is, I think she ought to be told all we know ourselves.'

"'That isn't much,' said Mrs. Dennison with a dying-away sort of sigh. She looked as if she might faint away again any minute. She was a real delicate-looking woman, but it turned out she was a good deal stronger than poor Mrs. Bird.

"'No, there isn't much we do know,' says Mrs. Bird, 'but what little there is she ought to know. I felt as if she ought to when she first came here.'

"'Well, I didn't feel quite right about it,' said Mrs. Dennison, 'but I kept hoping it might stop, and any way, that it might never trouble her, and you had put so much in the house, and we needed the money, and I didn't know but she might be nervous and think she couldn't come, and I didn't want to take a man boarder.'

"'And aside from the money, we were very anxious to have you come, my dear,' says Mrs. Bird.

"'Yes,' says Mrs. Dennison, 'we wanted the young company in the house; we were lonesome, and we both of us took a great liking to you the minute we set eyes on you.'

"And I guess they meant what they said, both of them. They were beautiful women, and nobody could be any kinder to me than they were, and I never blamed them for not telling me before, and, as they said, there wasn't really much to tell.

"They hadn't any sooner fairly bought the house, and moved into it, than they began to see and hear things. Mrs. Bird said they were sitting together in the sitting-room one evening when they heard it the first time. She said her sister was knitting lace (Mrs. Dennison made beautiful knitted lace) and she was reading the Missionary Herald (Mrs. Bird was very much interested in mission work), when all of a sudden they heard something. She heard it first and she laid down her Missionary Herald and listened, and then Mrs. Dennison she saw her listening and she drops her lace. 'What is it you are listening to, Abby?' says she. Then it came again and they both heard, and the cold shivers went down their backs to hear it, though they didn't know why. 'It's the cat, isn't it?' says Mrs. Bird.

"'It isn't any cat,' says Mrs. Dennison.

"'Oh, I guess it MUST be the cat; maybe she's got a mouse,' says Mrs. Bird, real cheerful, to calm down Mrs. Dennison, for she saw she was 'most scared to death, and she was always afraid of her fainting away. Then she opens the door and calls, 'Kitty, kitty, kitty!' They had brought their cat with them in a basket when they came to East Wilmington to live. It was a real handsome tiger cat, a tommy, and he knew a lot.

"Well, she called 'Kitty, kitty, kitty!' and sure enough the kitty came, and when he came in the door he gave a big yawl that didn't sound unlike what they had heard.

"'There, sister, here he is; you see it was the cat,' says Mrs. Bird. 'Poor kitty!'

"But Mrs. Dennison she eyed the cat, and she give a great screech.

"'What's that? What's that?' says she.

"'What's what?' says Mrs. Bird, pretending to herself that she didn't see what her sister meant.

"'Somethin's got hold of that cat's tail,' says Mrs. Dennison. 'Somethin's got hold of his tail. It's pulled straight out, an' he can't get away. Just hear him yawl!'

"'It isn't anything,' says Mrs. Bird, but even as she said that she could see a little hand holding fast to that cat's tail, and then the child seemed to sort of clear out of the dimness behind the hand, and the child was sort of laughing then, instead of looking sad, and she said that was a great deal worse. She said that laugh was the most awful and the saddest thing she ever heard.

"Well, she was so dumfounded that she didn't know what to do, and she couldn't sense at first that it was anything supernatural. She thought it must be one of the neighbour's children who had run away and was making free of their house, and was teasing their cat, and that they must be just nervous to feel so upset by it. So she speaks up sort of sharp.

"'Don't you know that you mustn't pull the kitty's tail?' says she. 'Don't you know you hurt the poor kitty, and she'll scratch you if you don't take care. Poor kitty, you mustn't hurt her.'

"And with that she said the child stopped pulling that cat's tail and went to stroking her just as soft and pitiful, and the cat put his back up and rubbed and purred as if he liked it. The cat never seemed a mite afraid, and that seemed queer, for I had always heard that animals were dreadfully afraid of ghosts; but then, that was a pretty harmless little sort of ghost.

"Well, Mrs. Bird said the child stroked that cat, while she and Mrs. Dennison stood watching it, and holding onto each other, for, no matter how hard they tried to think it was all right, it didn't look right. Finally Mrs. Dennison she spoke.

"'What's your name, little girl?' says she.

"Then the child looks up and stops stroking the cat, and says she can't find her mother, just the way she said it to me. Then Mrs. Dennison she gave such a gasp that Mrs. Bird thought she was going to faint away, but she didn't. 'Well, who is your mother?' says she. But the child just says again 'I can't find my mother—I can't find my mother.'

"'Where do you live, dear?' says Mrs. Bird.

"'I can't find my mother,' says the child.

"Well, that was the way it was. Nothing happened. Those two women stood there hanging onto each other, and the child stood in front of them, and they asked her questions, and everything she would say was: 'I can't find my mother.'

"Then Mrs. Bird tried to catch hold of the child, for she thought in spite of what she saw that perhaps she was nervous and it was a real child, only perhaps not quite right in its head, that had run away in her little nightgown after she had been put to bed.

"She tried to catch the child. She had an idea of putting a shawl around it and going out—she was such a little thing she could have carried her easy enough—and trying to find out to which of the neighbours she belonged. But the minute she moved toward the child there wasn't any child there; there was only that little voice seeming to come from nothing, saying 'I can't find my mother,' and presently that died away.

"Well, that same thing kept happening, or something very much the same. Once in awhile Mrs. Bird would be washing dishes, and all at once the child would be standing beside her with the dish-towel, wiping them. Of course, that was terrible. Mrs. Bird would wash the dishes all over. Sometimes she didn't tell Mrs. Dennison, it made her so nervous. Sometimes when they were making cake they would find the raisins all picked over, and sometimes little sticks of kindling-wood would be found laying beside the kitchen stove. They never knew when they would come across that child, and always she kept saying over and over that she couldn't find her mother. They never tried talking to her, except once in awhile Mrs. Bird would get desperate and ask her something, but the child never seemed to hear it; she always kept right on saying that she couldn't find her mother.

"After they had told me all they had to tell about their experience with the child, they told me about the house and the people that had lived there before they did. It seemed something dreadful had happened in that house. And the land agent had never let on to them. I don't think they would have bought it if he had, no matter how cheap it was, for even if folks aren't really afraid of anything, they don't want to live in houses where such dreadful things have happened that you keep thinking about them. I know after they told me I should never have stayed there another night, if I hadn't thought so much of them, no matter how comfortable I was made; and I never was nervous, either. But I stayed. Of course, it didn't happen in my room. If it had I could not have stayed."

"What was it?" asked Mrs. Emerson in an awed voice.

"It was an awful thing. That child had lived in the house with her father and mother two years before. They had come—or the father had—from a real good family. He had a good situation: he was a drummer for a big leather house in the city, and they lived real pretty, with plenty to do with. But the mother was a real wicked woman. She was as handsome as a picture, and they said she came from good sort of people enough in Boston, but she was bad clean through, though she was real pretty spoken and most everybody liked her. She used to dress out and make a great show, and she never seemed to take much interest in the child, and folks began to say she wasn't treated right.

"The woman had a hard time keeping a girl. For some reason one wouldn't stay. They would leave and then talk about her awfully, telling all kinds of things. People didn't believe it at first; then they began to. They said that the woman made that little thing, though she wasn't much over five years old, and small and babyish for her age, do most of the work, what there was done; they said the house used to look like a pig-sty when she didn't have help. They said the little thing used to stand on a chair and wash dishes, and they'd seen her carrying in sticks of wood most as big as she was many a time, and they'd heard her mother scolding her. The woman was a fine singer, and had a voice like a screech-owl when she scolded.

"The father was away most of the time, and when that happened he had been away out West for some weeks. There had been a married man hanging about the mother for some time, and folks had talked some; but they weren't sure there was anything wrong, and he was a man very high up, with money, so they kept pretty still for fear he would hear of it and make trouble for them, and of course nobody was sure, though folks did say afterward that the father of the child had ought to have been told.

"But that was very easy to say; it wouldn't have been so easy to find anybody who would have been willing to tell him such a thing as that, especially when they weren't any too sure. He set his eyes by his wife, too. They said all he seemed to think of was to earn money to buy things to deck her out in. And he about worshiped the child, too. They said he was a real nice man. The men that are treated so bad mostly are real nice men. I've always noticed that.

"Well, one morning that man that there had been whispers about was missing. He had been gone quite a while, though, before they really knew that he was missing, because he had gone away and told his wife that he had to go to New York on business and might be gone a week, and not to worry if he didn't get home, and not to worry if he didn't write, because he should be thinking from day to day that he might take the next train home and there would be no use in writing. So the wife waited, and she tried not to worry until it was two days over the week, then she run into a neighbour's and fainted dead away on the floor; and then they made inquiries and found out that he had skipped—with some money that didn't belong to him, too.

"Then folks began to ask where was that woman, and they found out by comparing notes that nobody had seen her since the man went away; but three or four women remembered that she had told them that she thought of taking the child and going to Boston to visit her folks, so when they hadn't seen her around, and the house shut, they jumped to the conclusion that was where she was. They were the neighbours that lived right around her, but they didn't have much to do with her, and she'd gone out of her way to tell them about her Boston plan, and they didn't make much reply when she did.

"Well, there was this house shut up, and the man and woman missing and the child. Then all of a sudden one of the women that lived the nearest remembered something. She remembered that she had waked up three nights running, thinking she heard a child crying somewhere, and once she waked up her husband, but he said it must be the Bisbees' little girl, and she thought it must be. The child wasn't well and was always crying. It used to have colic spells, especially at night. So she didn't think any more about it until this came up, then all of a sudden she did think of it. She told what she had heard, and finally folks began to think they had better enter that house and see if there was anything wrong.

"Well, they did enter it, and they found that child dead, locked in one of the rooms. (Mrs. Dennison and Mrs. Bird never used that room; it was a back bedroom on the second floor.)

"Yes, they found that poor child there, starved to death, and frozen, though they weren't sure she had frozen to death, for she was in bed with clothes enough to keep her pretty warm when she was alive. But she had been there a week, and she was nothing but skin and bone. It looked as if the mother had locked her into the house when she went away, and told her not to make any noise for fear the neighbours would hear her and find out that she herself had gone.

"Mrs. Dennison said she couldn't really believe that the woman had meant to have her own child starved to death. Probably she thought the little thing would raise somebody, or folks would try to get in the house and find her. Well, whatever she thought, there the child was, dead.

"But that wasn't all. The father came home, right in the midst of it; the child was just buried, and he was beside himself. And— he went on the track of his wife, and he found her, and he shot her dead; it was in all the papers at the time; then he disappeared. Nothing had been seen of him since. Mrs. Dennison said that she thought he had either made way with himself or got out of the country, nobody knew, but they did know there was something wrong with the house.

"'I knew folks acted queer when they asked me how I liked it when we first came here,' says Mrs. Dennison, 'but I never dreamed why till we saw the child that night.'

"I never heard anything like it in my life," said Mrs. Emerson, staring at the other woman with awestruck eyes.

"I thought you'd say so," said Mrs. Meserve. "You don't wonder that I ain't disposed to speak light when I hear there is anything queer about a house, do you?"

"No, I don't, after that," Mrs. Emerson said.

"But that ain't all," said Mrs. Meserve.

"Did you see it again?" Mrs. Emerson asked.

"Yes, I saw it a number of times before the last time. It was lucky I wasn't nervous, or I never could have stayed there, much as

I liked the place and much as I thought of those two women; they were beautiful women, and no mistake. I loved those women. I hope Mrs. Dennison will come and see me sometime.

"Well, I stayed, and I never knew when I'd see that child. I got so I was very careful to bring everything of mine upstairs, and not leave any little thing in my room that needed doing, for fear she would come lugging up my coat or hat or gloves or I'd find things done when there'd been no live being in the room to do them. I can't tell you how I dreaded seeing her; and worse than the seeing her was the hearing her say, 'I can't find my mother.' It was enough to make your blood run cold. I never heard a living child cry for its mother that was anything so pitiful as that dead one. It was enough to break your heart.

"She used to come and say that to Mrs. Bird oftener than to any one else. Once I heard Mrs. Bird say she wondered if it was possible that the poor little thing couldn't really find her mother in the other world, she had been such a wicked woman.

"But Mrs. Dennison told her she didn't think she ought to speak so nor even think so, and Mrs. Bird said she shouldn't wonder if she was right. Mrs. Bird was always very easy to put in the wrong. She was a good woman, and one that couldn't do things enough for other folks. It seemed as if that was what she lived on. I don't think she was ever so scared by that poor little ghost, as much as she pitied it, and she was 'most heartbroken because she couldn't do anything for it, as she could have done for a live child.

"'It seems to me sometimes as if I should die if I can't get that awful little white robe off that child and get her in some clothes and feed her and stop her looking for her mother,' I heard her say once, and she was in earnest. She cried when she said it. That wasn't long before she died.

"Now I am coming to the strangest part of it all. Mrs. Bird died very sudden. One morning—it was Saturday, and there wasn't any school—I went downstairs to breakfast, and Mrs. Bird wasn't there; there was nobody but Mrs. Dennison. She was pouring out the coffee when I came in. 'Why, where's Mrs. Bird?' says I.

"'Abby ain't feeling very well this morning,' says she; 'there isn't much the matter, I guess, but she didn't sleep very well, and her head aches, and she's sort of chilly, and I told her I thought she'd better stay in bed till the house gets warm.' It was a very cold morning.

"'Maybe she's got cold,' says I.

"'Yes, I guess she has,' says Mrs. Dennison. 'I guess she's got cold. She'll be up before long. Abby ain't one to stay in bed a minute longer than she can help.'

"Well, we went on eating our breakfast, and all at once a shadow flickered across one wall of the room and over the ceiling the way a shadow will sometimes when somebody passes the window outside. Mrs. Dennison and I both looked up, then out of the window; then Mrs. Dennison she gives a scream.

"'Why, Abby's crazy!' says she. 'There she is out this bitter cold morning, and—and—' She didn't finish, but she meant the child. For we were both looking out, and we saw, as plain as we ever saw anything in our lives, Mrs. Abby Bird walking off over the white snow-path with that child holding fast to her hand, nestling close to her as if she had found her own mother.

"'She's dead,' says Mrs. Dennison, clutching hold of me hard. 'She's dead; my sister is dead!'

"She was. We hurried upstairs as fast as we could go, and she was dead in her bed, and smiling as if she was dreaming, and one arm and hand was stretched out as if something had hold of it; and it couldn't be straightened even at the last—it lay out over her casket at the funeral."

"Was the child ever seen again?" asked Mrs. Emerson in a shaking voice.

"No," replied Mrs. Meserve; "that child was never seen again after she went out of the yard with Mrs. Bird."

THE YATES PRIDE

A ROMANCE

PART I

THE YATES PRIDE

Opposite Miss Eudora Yates's old colonial mansion was the perky modern Queen Anne residence of Mrs. Joseph Glynn. Mrs. Glynn had a daughter, Ethel, and an unmarried sister, Miss Julia Esterbrook. All three were fond of talking, and had many callers who liked to hear the feebly effervescent news of Wellwood. This afternoon three ladies were there: Miss Abby Simson, Mrs. John Bates, and Mrs. Edward Lee. They sat in the Glynn sitting-room, which shrilled with treble voices as if a flock of sparrows had settled therein.

The Glynn sitting-room was charming, mainly because of the quantity of flowering plants. Every window was filled with them, until the room seemed like a conservatory. Ivy, too, climbed over the pictures, and the mantel-shelf was a cascade of wandering Jew, growing in old china vases.

"Your plants are really wonderful, Mrs. Glynn," said Mrs. Bates, "but I don't see how you manage to get a glimpse of anything outside the house, your windows are so full of them."

"Maybe she can see and not be seen," said Abby Simson, who had a quick wit and a ready tongue.

Mrs. Joseph Glynn flushed a little. "I have not the slightest curiosity about my neighbors," she said, "but it is impossible to live just across the road from any house without knowing something of what is going on, whether one looks or not," said she, with dignity.

"Ma and I never look out of the windows from curiosity," said Ethel Glynn, with spirit. Ethel Glynn had a great deal of spirit, which was evinced in her personal appearance as well as her tongue.

She had an eye to the fashions; her sleeves were never out of date, nor was the arrangement of her hair.

"For instance," said Ethel, "we never look at the house opposite because we are at all prying, but we do know that that old maid has been doing a mighty queer thing lately."

"First thing you know you will be an old maid yourself, and then your stones will break your own glass house," said Abby Simson.

"Oh, I don't care," retorted Ethel. "Nowadays an old maid isn't an old maid except from choice, and everybody knows it. But it must have been different in Miss Eudora's time. Why, she is older than you are, Miss Abby."

"Just five years," replied Abby, unruffled, "and she had chances, and I know it."

"Why didn't she take them, then?"

"Maybe," said Abby, "girls had choice then as much as now, but I never could make out why she didn't marry Harry Lawton."

Ethel gave her head a toss. "Maybe," said she, "once in a while, even so long ago, a girl wasn't so crazy to get married as folks thought. Maybe she didn't want him."

"She did want him," said Abby. "A girl doesn't get so pale and peaked-looking for nothing as Eudora Yates did, after she had dismissed Harry Lawton and he had gone away, nor haunt the post-office as she used to, and, when she didn't get a letter, go away looking as if she would die."

"Maybe," said Ethel, "her folks were opposed."

"Nobody ever opposed Eudora Yates except her own self," replied Abby. "Her father was dead, and Eudora's ma thought the sun rose and set in her. She would never have opposed her if she had wanted to marry a foreign duke or the old Harry himself."

"I remember it perfectly," said Mrs. Joseph Glynn.

"So do I," said Julia Esterbrook.

"Don't see why you shouldn't. You were plenty old enough to have your memory in good working order if it was ever going to be," said Abby Simson.

"Well," said Ethel, "it is the funniest thing I ever heard of. If a girl wanted a man enough to go all to pieces over him, and he wanted her, why on earth didn't she take him?"

"Maybe they quarreled," ventured Mrs. Edward Lee, who was a mild, sickly-looking woman and seldom expressed an opinion.

"Well, that might have been," agreed Abby, "although Eudora always had the name of having a beautiful disposition."

"I have always found," said Mrs. Joseph Glynn, with an air of wisdom, "that it is the beautiful dispositions which are the most set the minute they get a start the wrong way. It is the always-flying-out people who are the easiest to get on with in the long run."

"Well," said Abby, "maybe that is so, but folks might get worn all to a frazzle by the flying-out ones before the long run. I'd rather take my chances with a woman like Eudora. She always seems just so, just as calm and sweet. When the Ames's barn, that was next to hers, burned down and the wind was her way, she just walked in and out of her house, carrying the things she valued most, and she looked like a picture—somehow she had got all dressed fit to make calls—and there wasn't a muscle of her face that seemed to move. Eudora Yates is to my mind the most beautiful woman in this town, old or young, I don't care who she is."

"I suppose," said Julia Esterbrook, "that she has a lot of money."

"I wonder if she has," said Mrs. John Bates.

The others stared at her. "What makes you think she hasn't?" Mrs. Glynn inquired, sharply.

"Nothing," said Mrs. Bates, and closed her thin lips. She would say no more, but the others had suspicions, because her husband, John Bates, was a wealthy business man.

"I can't believe she has lost her money," said Mrs. Glynn. "She wouldn't have been such a fool as to do what she has if she hadn't money."

"What has she done?" asked Mrs. Bates, eagerly.

"What has she done?" asked Abby, and Mrs. Lee looked up inquiringly.

The faces of Mrs. Glynn, her daughter, and her sister became important, full of sly and triumphant knowledge.

"Haven't you heard?" asked Mrs. Glynn.

"Yes, haven't you?" asked Ethel.

"Haven't any of you heard?" asked Julia Esterbrook.

"No," admitted Abby, rather feebly. "I don't know as I have."

"Do you mean about Eudora's going so often to the Lancaster girls' to tea?" asked Mrs. John Bates, with a slight bridle of possible knowledge.

"I heard of that," said Mrs. Lee, not to be outdone.

"Land, no," replied Mrs. Glynn. "Didn't she always go there? It isn't that. It is the most unheard-of thing she had done; but no woman, unless she had plenty of money to bring it up, would have done it."

"To bring what up?" asked Abby, sharply. Her eyes looked as small and bright as needles.

Julia regarded her with intense satisfaction. "What do women generally bring up?" said she.

"I don't know of anything they bring up, whether they have it or not, except a baby," retorted Abby, sharply.

Julia wilted a little; but her sister, Mrs. Glynn, was not perturbed. She launched her thunderbolt of news at once, aware that the critical moment had come, when the quarry of suspicion had left the bushes.

"She has adopted a baby," said she, and paused like a woman who had fired a gun, half scared herself and shrinking from the report.

Ethel seconded her mother. "Yes," said she, "Miss Eudora has adopted a baby, and she has a baby-carriage, and she wheels it out any time she takes a notion." Ethel's speech was of the nature of an after-climax. The baby-carriage weakened the situation.

The other women seized upon the idea of the carriage to cover their surprise and prevent too much gloating on the part of Mrs. Glynn, Ethel, and Julia.

"Is it a new carriage?" inquired Mrs. Lee.

"No, it looks like one that came over in the ark," retorted Mrs. Glynn. Then she repeated: "She has adopted a baby," but this time there was no effect of an explosion. However, the treble chorus rose high, "Where did she get the baby? Was it a boy or a girl? Why did she adopt it? Did it cry much?" and other queries, none of which Mrs. Glynn, Ethel, and Julia could answer very decidedly except the last. They all announced that the adopted baby was never heard to cry at all.

"Must be a very good child," said Abby.

"Must be a very healthy child," said Mrs. Lee, who had had experience with crying babies.

"Well, she has it, anyhow," said Mrs. Glynn.

Right upon the announcement came proof. The beautiful door of the old colonial mansion opposite was thrown open, and clumsy and cautious motion was evident. Presently a tall, slender woman came down the path between the box borders, pushing a baby-carriage. It was undoubtedly a very old carriage. It must have dated back to the fifties, if not the forties. It was made of wood, with a leather buggy-top, and was evidently very heavy.

Abby eyed it shrewdly. "If I am not mistaken," said she, "that is the very carriage Eudora herself was wheeled around in when she was a baby. I am almost sure I have seen that identical carriage before. When we were girls I used to go to the Yates house sometimes. Of course, it was always very formal, a little tea-party for Eudora, with her mother on hand, but I feel sure that I saw that carriage there one of those times.

"I suppose it cost a lot of money, in the time of it. The Yateses always got the very best for Eudora," said Julia. "And maybe Eudora goes about so little she doesn't realize how out of date the carriage is, but I should think it would be very heavy to wheel, especially if the baby is a good-sized one."

"It looks like a very large baby," said Ethel. "Of course, it is so rolled up we can't tell."

"Haven't you gone out and asked to see the baby?" said Abby.

"Would we dare unless Eudora Yates offered to show it?" said Julia, with a surprised air; and the others nodded assent. Then they all crowded to the front windows and watched from behind the screens of green flowering things. It was very early in the spring. Fairly hot days alternated with light frosts. The trees were touched with sprays of rose and gold and gold-green, but the wind still blew cold from the northern snows, and the occupant of Eudora's ancient carriage was presumably wrapped well to shelter it from harm. There was, in fact, nothing to be seen in the carriage, except a large roll of blue and white, as Eudora emerged from the yard and closed the iron gate of the tall fence behind her.

Through this fence pricked the evergreen box, and the deep yard was full of soft pastel tints of reluctantly budding trees and bushes. There was one deep splash of color from a yellow bush in full bloom.

Eudora paced down the sidewalk with a magnificent, stately gait. There was something rather magnificent in her whole appearance. Her skirts of old, but rich, black fabric swept about her long, advancing limbs; she held her black-bonneted head high, as if crowned. She pushed the cumbersome baby-carriage with no apparent effort. An ancient India shawl was draped about her sloping shoulders.

Eudora, as she passed the Glynn house, turned her face slightly, so that its pure oval was evident. She was now a beauty in late middle life. Her hair, of an indeterminate shade, swept in soft shadows over her ears; her features were regular; her expression was at once regal and gentle. A charm which was neither of youth nor of age reigned in her face; her grace had surmounted with triumphant ease the slope of every year. Eudora passed out of sight with the baby-carriage, lifting her proud lady-head under the soft droop of the spring boughs; and her inspectors, whom she had not seen, moved back from the Glynn windows with exclamations of astonishment.

"I wonder," said Abby, "whether she will have that baby call her ma or aunty."

Meantime Eudora passed down the village street until she reached the Lancaster house, about half a mile away on the same side. There dwelt the Misses Amelia and Anna Lancaster, who were about Eudora's age, and a widowed sister, Mrs. Sophia Willing, who was much older. The Lancaster house was also a colonial mansion, much after the fashion of Eudora's, but it showed signs of continued opulence. Eudora's, behind her trees and leafing vines, was gray for lack of paint. Some of the colonial ornamental details about porches and roof were sloughing off or had already disappeared. The Lancaster house gleamed behind its grove of evergreen trees as white and perfect as in its youth. The windows showed rich slants of draperies behind their green glister of old glass.

A gardener, with a boy assistant, was at work in the grounds when Eudora entered. He touched his cap. He was an old man who had lived with the Lancasters ever since Eudora could remember. He advanced toward her now. "Sha'n't Tommy push—the baby-carriage up to the house for you, Miss Eudora?" he said, in his cracked old voice.

Eudora flushed slightly, and, as if in response, the old man flushed, also. "No, I thank you, Wilson," she said, and moved on.

The boy, who was raking dry leaves, stood gazing at them with a shrewd, whimsical expression. He was the old man's grandson.

"Is that a boy or a girl kid, grandpa?" he inquired, when the gardener returned.

"Hold your tongue!" replied the old man, irascibly. Suddenly he seized the boy by his two thin little shoulders with knotted old hands.

"Look at here, Tommy, whatever you know, you keep your mouth shet, and whatever you don't know, you keep your mouth shet, if you know what's good for you," he said, in a fierce whisper.

The boy whistled and shrugged his shoulders loose. "You know I ain't goin' to tell tales, grandpa," he said, in a curiously manly fashion.

The old man nodded. "All right, Tommy. I don't believe you be, nuther, but you may jest as well git it through your head what's goin' to happen if you do."

"Ain't goin' to," returned the boy. He whistled charmingly as he raked the leaves. His whistle sounded like the carol of a bird.

Eudora pushed the carriage around to the side door, and immediately there was a fluttering rush of a slender woman clad in lavender down the steps. This woman first kissed Eudora with gentle fervor, then, with a sly look around and voice raised intentionally high, she lifted the blue and white roll from the carriage with the tenderest care. "Did the darling come to see his aunties?" she shrilled.

The old man and the boy in the front yard heard her distinctly. The old man's face was imperturbable. The boy grinned.

Two other women, all clad in lavender, appeared in the doorway. They also bent over the blue and white bundle. They also said something about the darling coming to see his aunties. Then there ensued the softest chorus of lady-laughter, as if at some hidden joke.

"Come in, Eudora dear," said Amelia Lancaster. "Yes, come in, Eudora dear," said Anna Lancaster. "Yes, come in, Eudora dear," said Sophia Willing.

Sophia looked much older than her sisters, but with that exception the resemblance between all three was startling. They always dressed exactly alike, too, in silken fabric of bluish lavender, like myrtle blossoms. Some of the poetical souls in the village called the Lancaster sisters "The ladies in lavender."

There was an astonishing change in the treatment of the blue and white bundle when the sisters and Eudora were in the stately old sitting-room, with its heavy mahogany furniture and its white-wainscoted calls. Amelia simply tossed the bundle into a corner of the sofa; then the sisters all sat in a loving circle around Eudora.

"Are you sure you are not utterly worn out, dear?" asked Amelia, tenderly; and the others repeated the question in exactly the same tone. The Lancaster sisters were not pretty, but all had charming expressions of gentleness and a dignified good-will and loving kindness. Their blue eyes beamed love at Eudora, and it was as if she sat encircled in a soul-ring of affection.

She responded, and her beautiful face glowed with tenderness and pleasure, and something besides, which was as the light of victory.

"I am not in the least tired, thank you, dears," she replied. "Why should I be tired? I am very strong."

Amelia murmured something about such hard work.

"I never thought it would be hard work taking care of a baby," replied Eudora, "and especially such a very light baby."

Something whimsical crept into Eudora's voice; something whimsical crept into the love-light of the other women's eyes. Again a soft ripple of mirth swept over them.

"Especially a baby who never cries," said Amelia.

"No, he never does cry," said Eudora, demurely.

They laughed again. Then Amelia rose and left the room to get the tea-things. The old serving-woman who had lived with them for many years was suffering from rheumatism, and was cared for by her daughter in the little cottage across the road from the Lancaster house. Her husband and grandson were the man and boy at work in the grounds. The three sisters took care of themselves and their house with the elegant ease and lack of fluster of gentlewomen born and bred. Miss Amelia, bringing in the tea-tray, was an unclassed being, neither maid nor mistress, but outranking either. She had tied on a white apron. She bore the silver tray with an ease which bespoke either nerve or muscle in her lace-draped arms.

She poured the tea, holding the silver pot high and letting the amber fluid trickle slowly, and the pearls and diamonds on her thin hands shone dully. Sophia passed little china plates and fringed napkins, and Anna a silver basket with golden squares of sponge-cake.

The ladies ate and drank, and the blue and white bundle on the sofa remained motionless. Eudora, after she had finished her tea, leaned back gracefully in her chair, and her dark eyes gleamed with its mild stimulus. She remained an hour or more. When she went out, Amelia slipped an envelope into her hand and at the same time embraced and kissed her. Sophia and Anna followed her example. Eudora opened her mouth as if to speak, but smiled instead, a fond, proud smile. During the last fifteen minutes of her stay Amelia had slipped out of the room with the blue and white bundle. Now she brought it out and laid it carefully in the carriage.

"We are always so glad to see you, dearest Eudora," said she, "but you understand—"

"Yes," said Sophia, "you understand, Eudora dear, that there is not the slightest haste."

Eudora nodded, and her long neck seemed to grow longer.

When she was stepping regally down the path, Amelia said in a hasty whisper to Sophia: "Did you tell her?"

Sophia shook her head. "No, sister."

"I didn't know but you might have, while I was out of the room."

"I did not," said Sophia. She looked doubtfully at Amelia, then at Anna, and doubt flashed back and forth between the three pairs of blue eyes for a second. Then Sophia spoke with authority, because she was the only one of them all who had entered the estate of matrimony, and had consequently obvious cognizance of such matters.

"I think," said she, "that Eudora should be told that Harry Lawton has come back and is boarding at the Wellwood Inn."

"You think," faltered Amelia, "that it is possible she might meet him unexpectedly?"

"I certainly do think so. And she might show her feelings in a way which she would ever afterward regret."

"You think, then, that she—"

Sophia gave her sister a look. Amelia fled after Eudora and the baby-carriage. She overtook her at the gate. She laid her hand on Eudora's arm, draped with India shawl.

"Eudora!" she gasped.

Eudora turned her serene face and regarded her questioningly.

"Eudora," said Amelia, "have you heard of anybody's coming to stay at the inn lately?"

"No," replied Eudora, calmly. "Why, dear?"

"Nothing, only, Eudora, a dear and old friend of yours, of ours, is there, so I hear."

Eudora did not inquire who the old friend might be. "Really?" she remarked. Then she said, "Goodby, Amelia dear," and resumed her progress with the baby-carriage.

PART II

"She never even asked who it was," Amelia reported to her sisters, when she had returned to the house. "Because she knew," replied Sophia, sagely; "there has never been any old friend but that one old friend to come back into Eudora Yates's life."

"Has he come back into her life, I wonder?" said Amelia.

"What did he return to Wellwood for if he didn't come for that? All his relatives are gone. He never married. Yes, he has come back to see Eudora and marry her, if she will have him. No man who ever loved Eudora would ever get over loving her. And he will not be shocked when he sees her. She is no more changed than a beautiful old statue."

"HE is changed, though," said Amelia. "I saw him the other day. He didn't see me, and I would hardly have known him. He has grown stout, and his hair is gray."

"Eudora's hair is gray," said Sophia.

"Yes, but you can see the gold through Eudora's gray. It just looks as if a shadow was thrown over it. It doesn't change her. Harry Lawton's gray hair does change him."

"If," said Anna, sentimentally, "Eudora thinks Harry's hair turned gray for love of her, you can trust her or any woman to see the gold through it."

"Harry's hair was never gold—just an ordinary brown," said Amelia. "Anyway, the Lawtons turned gray young."

"She won't think of that at all," said Sophia.

"I wonder why Eudora always avoided him so, years ago," said Amelia.

"Why doesn't a girl in a field of daisies stop to pick one, which she never forgets?" said Sophia. "Eudora had so many chances, and

I don't think her heart was fixed when she was very young; at least, I don't think it was fixed so she knew it."

"I wonder," said Amelia, "if he will go and call on her."

Amelia privately wished that she lived near enough to know if Harry Lawton did call. She, as well as Mrs. Joseph Glynn, would have enjoyed watching out and knowing something of the village happenings, but the Lancaster house was situated so far from the road, behind its grove of trees, that nothing whatever could be seen.

"I doubt if Eudora tells, if he does call—that is, not unless something definite happens," said Anna.

"No," remarked Amelia, sadly. "Eudora is a dear, but she is very silent with regard to her own affairs."

"She ought to be," said Sophia, with her married authority. She was, to her sisters, as one who had passed within the shrine and was dignifiedly silent with regard to its intimate mysteries.

"I suppose so," assented Anna, with a soft sigh. Amelia sighed also. Then she took the tea-tray out of the room. She had to make some biscuits for supper.

Meantime Eudora was pacing homeward with the baby-carriage. Her serene face was a little perturbed. Her oval cheeks were flushed, and her mouth now and then trembled. She had, if she followed her usual course, to pass the Wellwood Inn, but she could diverge, and by taking a side street and walking a half-mile farther reach home without coming in sight of the inn. She did so today.

When she reached the side street she turned rather swiftly and gave a little sigh of relief. She was afraid that she might meet Harry Lawton. It was a lonely way. There was a brook on one side, bordered thickly with bushy willows which were turning gold-green. On the other side were undulating pasture-lands on which grazed a few sheep. There were no houses until she reached the turn which would lead back to the main street, on which her home was located.

Eudora was about midway of this street when she saw a man approaching. He was a large man clad in gray, and he was swinging an umbrella. Somehow the swing of that umbrella, even from a distance, gave an impression of embarrassment and boyish hesitation. Eudora did not know him at first. She had expected to see the same Harry Lawton who had gone away. She did not expect to see a stout, middle-aged man, but a slim youth.

However, as they drew nearer each other, she knew; and curiously enough it was that swing of the tightly furled umbrella which gave her the clue. She knew Harry because of that. It was a little boyish trick which had survived time. It was too late for her to draw back, for he had seen her, and Eudora was keenly alive to the indignity of abruptly turning and scuttling away with the tail of her black silk swishing, her India shawl trailing, and the baby-carriage bumping over the furrows. She continued, and Harry Lawton continued, and they met.

Harry Lawton had known Eudora at once. She looked the same to him as when she had been a girl, and he looked the same to her when he spoke.

"Hullo, Eudora," said Harry Lawton, in a ludicrously boyish fashion. His face flushed, too, like a boy. He extended his hand like a boy. The man, seen near at hand, was a boy. In reality he himself had not changed. A few layers of flesh and a change of color-cells do not make another man. He had always been a simple, sincere, friendly soul, beloved of men and women alike, and he was that now. Eudora held out her hand, and her eyes fell before the eyes of the man, in an absurd fashion for such a stately creature as she. But the man himself acted like a great happy overgrown school-boy.

"Hullo, Eudora," he said again.

"Hullo," said she, falteringly.

It was inconceivable that they should meet in such wise after the years of separation and longing which they had both undergone; but each took refuge, as it were, in a long-past youth, even childhood, from the fierce tension of age. When they were both children they had been accustomed to pass each other on the village street with exactly such salutation, and now both reverted to it. The tall, regal woman in her India shawl and the stout, middle-aged man had both stepped back to their vantage-ground of springtime to meet.

However, after a moment, Eudora reasserted herself. "I only heard a short time ago that you were here," she said, in her usual even voice. The fair oval of her face was as serene and proud toward the man as the face of the moon.

The man swung his umbrella, then began prodding the ground with it. "Hullo, Eudora," he said again; then he added: "How are you, anyway? Fine and well?"

"I am very well, thank you," said Eudora. "So you have come home to Wellwood after all this time?"

The man made an effort and recovered himself, although his handsome face was burning.

"Yes," he remarked, with considerable ease and dignity, to which he had a right, for Harry Lawton had not made a failure of his life, even though it had not included Eudora and a fulfilled dream.

"Yes," he continued, "I had some leisure; in fact, I have this spring retired from business; and I thought I would have a look at the old place. Very little changed I am happy to find it."

"Yes, it is very little changed," assented Eudora; "at least, it seems so to me, but it is not for a life-long dweller in any place to judge of change. It is for the one who goes and returns after many years."

There was a faint hint of proud sadness in Eudora's voice as she spoke the last two words.

"It has been many years," said Lawton, gravely, "and I wonder if it has seemed so to you."

Eudora held her head proudly. "Time passes swiftly," said she, tritely.

"But sometimes it may seem long in the passing, however swift," said Lawton, "though I suppose it has not to you. You look just the same," he added, regarding her admiringly.

Eudora flushed a little. "I must be changed," she murmured.

"Not a bit. I would have known you anywhere. But I—"

"I knew you the minute you spoke."

"Did you?" he asked, eagerly. "I was afraid I had grown so stout you would not remember me at all. Queer how a man will grow stout. I am not such a big eater, either, and I have worked hard, and—well, I might have been worse off, but I must say I have seen men who seemed to me happier, though I have made the best of things. I always did despise a flunk. But you! I heard you had adopted a baby," he said, with a sudden glance at the blue and white bundle in the carriage, "and I thought you were mighty sensible. When people grow old they want young people growing around them, staffs for old age, you know, and all that sort of thing. Don't know but I should have adopted a boy myself if it hadn't been for—"

The man stopped, and his face was pink. Eudora turned her face slightly away.

"By the way," said the man, in a suddenly hushed voice, "I suppose the kid you've got there is asleep. Wouldn't do to wake him?"

"I think I had better not," replied Eudora, in a hesitating voice. She began to walk along, and Harry Lawton fell into step beside her.

"I suppose it isn't best to wake up babies; makes them cross, and they cry," he said. "Say, Eudora, is he much trouble?"

"Very little," replied Eudora, still in that strange voice.

"Doesn't keep you awake nights?"

"Oh no."

"Because if he does, I really think you should have a nurse. I don't think you ought to lose sleep taking care of him."

"I do not."

"Well, I was mighty glad when I heard you had adopted him. I suppose you made sure about his parentage, where he hailed from and what sort of people?"

"Oh yes." Eudora was very pale.

"That's right. Maybe some time you will tell me all about it. I am coming over Thursday to have a look at the youngster. I have to go to the city on business tomorrow and can't get back until Thursday. I was coming over tonight to call on you, but I have a man coming to the inn this evening—he called me up on the telephone just now—one of the men who have taken my place in the business; and as long as I have met you I will just walk along with you, and come Thursday. I suppose the baby won't be likely to wake up just yet, and when he does you'll have to get his supper and put him to bed. Is that the way the rule goes?"

Eudora nodded in a shamed, speechless sort of way.

"All right. I'll come Thursday-but say, look here, Eudora. This is a quiet road, not a soul in sight, just like an outdoor room to ourselves. Why shouldn't I know now just as well as wait? Say, Eudora, you know how I used to feel about you. Well, it has lasted all these years. There has never been another woman I even cared to look at. You are alone, except for that baby, and I am alone. Eudora—"

The man hesitated. His flushed face had paled. Eudora paced silently and waveringly at his side.

"Eudora," the man went on, "you know you always used to run away from me—never gave me a chance to really ask; and I thought you didn't care. But somehow I have wondered—perhaps because you never got married—if you didn't quite mean it, if you didn't quite know your own mind. You'll think I'm a conceited ass, but I'm not a bad sort, Eudora. I would be as good to you as I know how, and—we could bring him up together." He pointed to the carriage. "I have plenty of money. We could do anything we wanted to do for him, and we should not have to live alone. Say, Eudora, you may not think it's the thing for a man to own up to, but, hang it all! I'm alone, and I don't want to face the rest of my life alone. Eudora, do you think you could make up your mind to marry me, after all?"

They had reached the turn in the road. Just beyond rose the stately pile of the old Yates mansion. Eudora stood still and gave one desperate look at her lover. "I will let you know Thursday," she gasped. Then she was gone, trundling the baby-carriage with incredible speed.

"But, Eudora—"

"I must go," she called back, faintly. The man stood staring after the hurrying figure with its swishing black skirts and its flying points of rich India shawl, and he smiled happily and tenderly. That evening at the inn his caller, a young fellow just married and beaming with happiness, saw an answering beam in the older man's face. He broke off in the midst of a sentence and stared at him.

"Don't give me away until I tell you to, Ned," he said, "but I don't know but I am going to follow your example."

"My example?"

"Yes, going to get married."

The young man gasped. A look of surprise, of amusement, then of generous sympathy came over his face. He grasped Lawton's hand.

"Who is she?"

"Oh, a woman I wanted more than anything in the world when I was about your age."

"Then she isn't young?"

"She is better than young."

"Well," agreed the young man, "being young and pretty is not everything."

"Pretty!" said Harry Lawton, scornfully, "pretty! She is a great beauty."

"And not young?"

"She is a great beauty, and better than young, because time has not touched her beauty, and you can see for yourself that it lasts."

The young man laughed. "Oh, well," he said, with a tender inflection, "I dare say that my Amy will look like that to me."

"If she doesn't you don't love her," said Lawton. "But my Eudora IS that."

"That is a queer-sounding Greek name."

"She is Greek, like her name. Such beauty never grows old. She stands on her pedestal, and time only looks at her to love her."

"I thought you were a business man as hard as nails," said the young man, wonderingly. Lawton laughed.

When Thursday came, Lawton, carefully dressed and carrying a long tissue-paper package, evidently of roses, approached the Yates house. It was late in the afternoon. There had been a warm day, and the trees were clouds of green and more bushes had blossomed. Eudora had put on a green silk dress of her youth. The revolving fashions had made it very passable, and the fabric was as beautiful as ever.

When Lawton presented her with the roses she pinned one in the yellowed lace which draped her bodice and put the rest in a great china vase on the table. The roses were very fragrant, and immediately the whole room was possessed by them.

A tiny, insistent cry came from a corner, and Lawton and Eudora turned toward it. There stood the old wooden cradle in which Eudora had been rocked to sleep, but over the clumsy hood Eudora had tacked a fall of rich old lace and a great bow of soft pink satin.

"He is waking up," said the man, in a hushed, almost reverent voice.

Eudora nodded. She went toward the cradle, and the man followed. She lifted the curtain of lace, and there became visible little feebly waving pink arms and hands, like tentacles of love, and a little puckered pink face which was at once ugly and divinely beautiful.

"A fine boy," said the man. The baby made a grimace at him which was hideous but lovely.

"I do believe he thinks he knows you," said Eudora, foolishly.

The baby made a little nestling motion, and its creasy eyelids dropped.

"Looks to me as if he was going to sleep again," said Lawton, in a whisper. Eudora jogged the cradle gently with her foot, and both were still. Then Eudora dropped the lace veil over the cradle again and moved softly away.

Lawton followed her. "I haven't my answer yet, Eudora," he whispered, leaning over her shoulder as she moved.

"Come into the other room," she murmured, "or we shall wake the baby." Her voice was softly excited.

Eudora led the way into the parlor, upon whose walls hung some really good portraits and whose furnishings still merited the adjective magnificent. There had been opulence in the Yates family; and in this room, which had been conserved, there was still undimmed and unfaded evidence of it. Eudora drew aside a brocade curtain and sat down on an embroidered satin sofa. Lawton sat beside her.

"This room looks every whit as grand as it used to look to me when I was a boy," he said.

"It has hardly been opened, except to have it cleaned, since you went away," replied Eudora, "and no wear has come upon it."

"And everything was rather splendid to begin with, and has lasted. And so were you, Eudora, and you have lasted. Well, what about my answer, dear girl?"

"You have to hear something first."

Lawton laughed. "A confession?"

Eudora held her head proudly. "No, not exactly," said she. "I am not sure that I have ever had anything to confess."

"You never were sure, you proud creature."

"I am not now. I never intended to deceive you, but you were deceived. I did intend to deceive others, others who had no right to know. I do not feel that I owe them any explanation. I do owe you one, although I do not feel that I have done anything wrong. Still, I cannot allow you to remain deceived."

"Well, what is it, dear?"

Eudora looked at him. "You remember that afternoon when you met me with the baby-carriage?"

"Well, I should think so. My memory has not failed me in three days."

"You thought I had a baby in that carriage."

"Of course I did."

"There wasn't a baby in the carriage."

"Well, what on earth was it, then? A cat?"

Eudora, if possible, looked prouder. "It was a package of soiled linen from the Lancaster girls."

"Oh, good heavens, Eudora!"

"Yes," said Eudora, proudly. "I lost nearly everything when that railroad failed. I had enough left to pay the taxes, and that was all. After I had used a small sum in the savings-bank there was nothing. One day I went over to the Lancasters', and I—well, I had not had much to eat for several days. I was a little faint, and—"

"Eudora, you poor, darling girl!"

"And the Lancaster girls found out," continued Eudora, calmly. "They gave me something to eat, and I suppose I ate as if I were famished. I was."

"Eudora!"

"And they wanted to give me money, but I would not take it, and they had been trying to find a laundress for their finer linen— their old serving-woman was ill. They could find one for the heavier things, but they are very particular, and I was sure I could manage, and so I begged them to let me have the work, and they did, and overpaid me, I fear. And I—I knew very well how many spying eyes were about, and I thought of my proud father and my proud mother and grandmother, and perhaps I was proud, too. You know they talk about the Yates pride. It was not so much because I was ashamed of doing honest work as because I did resent those prying eyes and tattling tongues, and so I said nothing, but I did go back and forth in broad daylight with the linen wrapped up in the old blue and white blanket, in my old carriage, and they thought what they thought."

Eudora laughed faintly. She had a gentle humor. "It was somewhat laughable, too," she observed. "The Lancaster girls and I have had our little jests over it, but I felt that I could not deceive you."

Lawton looked bewildered. "But that is a real baby in there," he said, jerking an elbow toward the other room.

"Oh yes," replied Eudora. "I adopted him yesterday. I went to the Children's Home in Elmfield. Amelia Lancaster went with me. Wilson drove us over. I know a nurse there. She took care of mother in her last illness. And I adopted this baby; at least, I am going to. He comes of respectable people, and his parents are dead. His mother died when he was born. He is healthy, and I thought him a beautiful baby."

"Yes, he is," assented Lawton, but he still looked somewhat perplexed. "But why did you hurry off so and get him, Eudora?" said he.

"I thought from what you said that day that you would be disappointed when you found out I had only the Lancaster linen and not a real baby," said Eudora with her calm, grand air and with no trace of a smile.

"Then that means that you say yes, Eudora?"

For the first time Eudora gave a startled glance at him. "Didn't you know?" she gasped.

"How should I? You had not said yes really, dear."

"Do you think," said Eudora Yates, "that I am not too proud to allow you to ask me if my answer were not yes?"

"So that is the reason you always ran away from me, years ago, so that I never had a chance to ask you?"

"Of course," said Eudora. "No woman of my family ever allows a declaration which she does not intend to accept. I was always taught that by my mother."

Then a small but insistent cry rent the air. "The baby is awake!" cried Eudora, and ran, or, rather, paced swiftly—Eudora had been taught never to run—and Lawton followed. It was he who finally quieted the child, holding the little thing in his arms.

But the baby, before that, cried so long and lustily that all the women in the Glynn house opposite were on the alert, and also some of the friends who were calling there. Abby Simson was one.

"Harry Lawton has been there over an hour now," said Abby, while the wailing continued, "and I know as well as I want to that there will be a wedding."

"I wonder he doesn't object to that adopted baby," said Julia Esterbrook.

"I know one thing," said Abby Simson. "It must be a boy baby, it hollers so."

CPSIA information can be obtained at www.ICGtesting.com
Printed in the USA
LVOW041417150112

263935LV00001B/44/A